TALES OF MYSTER

CW00346441

THE BELL IN THE FOG
and Other Stories

THE BELL IN THE FOG

and Other Stories

Gertrude Atherton

WORDSWORTH EDITIONS

In loving memory of
MICHAEL TRAYLER
the founder of Wordsworth Editions

2

Readers who are interested in other titles from
Wordsworth Editions are invited to visit our website at
www.wordsworth-editions.com

For our latest list and a full mail-order service contact
Bibliophile Books, 5 Thomas Road, London E14 7BN
Tel: +44 0207 515 9222 Fax: +44 0207 538 4115
e-mail: orders@bibliophilebooks.com

This edition published 2006 by
Wordsworth Editions Limited
8B East Street, Ware, Hertfordshire SG12 9HJ

ISBN 978-1-84022-540-2

© Wordsworth Editions Limited 2006

Wordsworth® is a registered trademark of
Wordsworth Editions Limited

All rights reserved. This publication may not be
reproduced, stored in a retrieval system or
transmitted in any form or by any means, electronic,
mechanical, photocopying, recording or otherwise,
without the prior permission of the publishers.

Typeset in Great Britain by Antony Gray
Printed by Clays Ltd, St Ives plc

CONTENTS

To the Master
HENRY JAMES

THE BELL IN THE FOG

The Bell in the Fog

I

The great author had realised one of the dreams of his ambitious youth, the possession of an ancestral hall in England. It was not so much the good American's reverence for ancestors that inspired the longing to consort with the ghosts of an ancient line, as artistic appreciation of the mellowness, the dignity, the aristocratic aloofness of walls that have sheltered, and furniture that has embraced, generations and generations of the dead. To mere wealth, only his astute and incomparably modern brain yielded respect; his ego raised its goose-flesh at the sight of rooms furnished with a single check, conciliatory as the taste might be. The dumping of the old interiors of Europe into the glistening shells of the United States not only roused him almost to passionate protest, but offended his patriotism – which he classified among his unworked ideals. The average American was not an artist, therefore he had no excuse for even the affectation of cosmopolitanism. Heaven knew he was national enough in everything else, from his accent to his lack of repose; let his surroundings be in keeping.

Orth had left the United States soon after his first successes, and, his art being too great to be confounded with locality, he had long since ceased to be spoken of as an American author. All civilised Europe furnished stages for his puppets, and, if never picturesque nor impassioned, his originality was as overwhelming as his style. His subtleties might not always be understood – indeed, as a rule, they were not – but the musical mystery of his language and the penetrating charm of his lofty and cultivated mind induced raptures in the initiated, forever denied to those who failed to appreciate him.

His following was not a large one, but it was very distinguished. The aristocracies of the earth gave to it; and not to understand and admire Ralph Orth was deliberately to relegate oneself to the ranks. But the elect are few, and they frequently subscribe to the circulating libraries; on the Continent, they buy the Tauchnitz edition; and had not Mr Orth inherited a sufficiency of ancestral dollars to enable him to keep rooms in Jermyn Street, and the wardrobe of an Englishman of leisure, he might have been forced to consider the tastes of the middle-class at a desk in Hampstead. But, as it mercifully was, the fashionable and exclusive sets of London knew and sought him. He was too wary to become a fad, and too sophisticated to grate or bore; consequently, his popularity continued evenly from year to year, and long since he had come to be regarded as one of them. He was not keenly addicted to sport, but he could handle a gun, and all men respected his dignity and breeding. They cared less for his books than women did, perhaps because patience is not a characteristic of their sex. I am alluding, however, in this instance, to men-of-the-world. A group of young literary men – and one or two women – put him on a pedestal and kissed the earth before it. Naturally, they imitated him, and as this flattered him, and he had a kindly heart deep among the cere-cloths of his formalities, he sooner or later wrote 'appreciations' of them all, which nobody living could understand, but which owing to the subtitle and signature answered every purpose.

With all this, however, he was not utterly content. From the 12th of August until late in the winter – when he did not go to Homburg and the Riviera – he visited the best houses in England, slept in state chambers, and meditated in historic parks; but the country was his one passion, and he longed for his own acres.

He was turning fifty when his great-aunt died and made him her heir: 'as a poor reward for his immortal services to literature', read the will of this phenomenally appreciative relative. The estate was a large one. There was a rush for his books; new editions were announced. He smiled with cynicism, not unmixed with sadness; but he was very grateful for the money, and as soon as his fastidious taste would permit he bought him a country seat.

The place gratified all his ideals and dreams – for he had romanced about his sometime English possession as he had never dreamed of woman. It had once been the property of the Church, and the ruin of cloister and chapel above the ancient wood was sharp against the low pale sky. Even the house itself was Tudor, but wealth from generation to generation had kept it in repair; and the lawns were as velvety, the hedges as rigid, the trees as aged as any in his own works. It was not a castle nor a great property, but it was quite perfect; and for a long while he felt like a bridegroom on a succession of honeymoons. He often laid his hand against the rough ivied walls in a lingering caress.

After a time, he returned the hospitalities of his friends, and his invitations, given with the exclusiveness of his great distinction, were never refused. Americans visiting England eagerly sought for letters to him; and if they were sometimes benumbed by that cold and formal presence, and awed by the silences of Chillingsworth – the few who entered there – they thrilled in anticipation of verbal triumphs, and forthwith bought an entire set of his books. It was characteristic that they dared not ask him for his autograph.

Although women invariably described him as 'brilliant', a few men affirmed that he was gentle and lovable, and any one of them was well content to spend weeks at Chillingsworth with no other companion. But, on the whole, he was rather a lonely man.

It occurred to him how lonely he was one gay June morning when the sunlight was streaming through his narrow windows, illuminating tapestries and armour, the family portraits of the young profligate from whom he had made this splendid purchase, dusting its gold on the black wood of wainscot and floor. He was in the gallery at the moment, studying one of his two favourite portraits, a gallant little lad in the green costume of Robin Hood. The boy's expression was imperious and radiant, and he had that perfect beauty which in any disposition appealed so powerfully to the author. But as Orth stared today at the brilliant youth, of whose life he knew nothing, he suddenly became aware of a human stirring at the foundations of his aesthetic pleasure.

'I wish he were alive and here,' he thought, with a sigh. 'What a jolly little companion he would be! And this fine old mansion would make a far more complementary setting for him than for me.'

He turned away abruptly, only to find himself face to face with the portrait of a little girl who was quite unlike the boy, yet so perfect in her own way, and so unmistakably painted by the same hand, that he had long since concluded they had been brother and sister. She was angelically fair, and, young as she was – she could not have been more than six years old – her dark-blue eyes had a beauty of mind which must have been remarkable twenty years later. Her pouting mouth was like a little scarlet serpent, her skin almost transparent, her pale hair fell waving – not curled with the orthodoxy of childhood – about her tender bare shoulders. She wore a long white frock, and clasped tightly against her breast a doll far more gorgeously arrayed than herself. Behind her were the ruins and the woods of Chillingsworth.

Orth had studied this portrait many times, for the sake of an art which he understood almost as well as his own; but today he saw only the lovely child. He forgot even the boy in the intensity of this new and personal absorption.

'Did she live to grow up, I wonder?' he thought. 'She should have made a remarkable, even a famous woman, with those eyes and that brow, but – could the spirit within that ethereal frame stand the enlightenments of maturity? Would not that mind – purged, perhaps, in a long probation from the dross of other existences – flee in disgust from the commonplace problems of a woman's life? Such perfect beings should die while they are still perfect. Still, it is possible that this little girl, whoever she was, was idealised by the artist, who painted into her his own dream of exquisite childhood.'

Again he turned away impatiently. 'I believe I am rather fond of children,' he admitted. 'I catch myself watching them on the street when they are pretty enough. Well, who does not like them?' he added, with some defiance.

He went back to his work; he was chiselling a story which was to be the foremost excuse of a magazine as yet unborn. At the end of half an hour he threw down his wondrous instrument – which looked not unlike an ordinary pen – and making no attempt to disobey the desire that possessed him, went back to the gallery. The dark splendid boy, the angelic little girl were all he saw – even of the several children in that roll-call of the past – and they seemed to look straight down his eyes into depths where the fragmentary ghosts of unrecorded ancestors gave faint musical response.

'The dead's kindly recognition of the dead,' he thought. 'But I wish these children were alive.'

For a week he haunted the gallery, and the children haunted him. Then he became impatient and angry. 'I am mooning like a barren woman,' he exclaimed. 'I must take the briefest way of getting those youngsters off my mind.'

With the help of his secretary, he ransacked the library, and finally brought to light the gallery catalogue which had been named in the inventory. He discovered that his children were the Viscount Tancred and the Lady Blanche Mortlake, son and daughter of the second Earl of Teignmouth. Little wiser than before, he sat down at once and wrote to the present earl, asking for some account of the lives of the children. He awaited the answer with more restlessness than he usually permitted himself, and took long walks, ostentatiously avoiding the gallery.

'I believe those youngsters have obsessed me,' he thought, more than once. 'They certainly are beautiful enough, and the last time I looked at them in that waning light they were fairly alive. Would that they were, and scampering about this park.'

Lord Teignmouth, who was intensely grateful to him, answered promptly.

'I am afraid,' he wrote, 'that I don't know much about my ancestors – those who didn't do something or other; but I have a vague remembrance of having been told by an aunt of mine, who lives on the family traditions – she isn't married – that the little chap was drowned in the river, and that the little girl died too – I mean when she was a little girl – wasted away, or something – I'm such a beastly idiot about expressing myself, that I wouldn't dare to write to you at all if you weren't really great. That is actually all I can tell you, and I am afraid the painter was their only biographer.'

The author was gratified that the girl had died young, but grieved for the boy. Although he had avoided the gallery of late, his practised imagination had evoked from the throngs of history the high-handed and brilliant, surely adventurous career of the third Earl of Teignmouth. He had pondered upon the deep delights of directing such a mind and character, and had caught himself envying the dust that was older still. When he read of the lad's early death, in spite of his regret that such promise should have come to naught, he admitted to a secret thrill of satisfaction that the boy had so soon ceased to belong to anyone. Then he smiled with both sadness and humour.

'What an old fool I am!' he admitted. 'I believe I not only wish those children were alive, but that they were my own.'

The frank admission proved fatal. He made straight for the gallery. The boy, after the interval of separation, seemed more spiritedly alive than ever, the little girl to suggest, with her faint appealing smile, that she would like to be taken up and cuddled.

'I must try another way,' he thought, desperately, after that long communion. 'I must write them out of me.'

He went back to the library and locked up the *tour de force* which had ceased to command his classic faculty. At once, he began to write the story of the brief lives of the children, much to the amazement of that faculty, which was little accustomed to the simplicities. Nevertheless, before he had written three chapters, he knew that he was at work upon a masterpiece – and more: he was experiencing a pleasure so keen that once and again his hand trembled, and he saw the page through a mist. Although his characters had always been objective to himself and his more patient readers, none knew better than he – a man of no delusions – that they were so remote and exclusive as barely to escape being mere mentalities; they were never the pulsing living creations of the more full-blooded genius. But he had been content to have it so. His creations might find and leave him cold, but he had known his highest satisfaction in chiselling the statuettes, extracting subtle and elevating harmonies, while combining words as no man of his tongue had combined them before.

But the children were not statuettes. He had loved and brooded over them long ere he had thought to tuck them into his pen, and on its first stroke they danced out alive. The old mansion echoed with their laughter, with their delightful and original pranks. Mr Orth knew nothing of children, therefore all the pranks he invented were as original as his faculty. The little girl clung to his hand or knee as they both followed the adventurous course of their common idol, the boy. When Orth realised how alive they were, he opened each room of his home to them in turn, that evermore he might have sacred and poignant memories with all parts of the stately mansion where he must dwell alone to the end. He selected their bedrooms, and hovered over them – not through infantile disorders, which were beyond even his imagination – but through those painful intervals incident upon the enterprising spirit of the boy and the devoted obedience of the girl to fraternal command. He ignored the second Lord Teignmouth; he was himself their father, and he admired himself extravagantly for the first time; art had chastened him long since. Oddly enough, the children had no mother, not even the memory of one.

He wrote the book more slowly than was his wont, and spent delightful hours pondering upon the chapter of the morrow. He looked forward to the conclusion with a sort of terror, and made up his mind that when the inevitable last word was written he should start at once for Homburg. Incalculable times a day he went to the gallery, for he no longer had any desire to write the children out of his mind, and his eyes hungered for them. They were his now. It was with an effort that he sometimes humorously reminded himself that another man had fathered them, and that their little skeletons were under the choir of the chapel. Not even for peace of mind would he have descended into the vaults of the lords of Chillingsworth and looked upon the marble effigies of his children.

Nevertheless, when in a superhumorous mood, he dwelt upon his high satisfaction in having been enabled by his great-aunt to purchase all that was left of them.

For two months he lived in his fool's paradise, and then he knew that the book must end. He nerved himself to nurse the little girl through her wasting illness, and when he clasped her hands, his own shook, his knees trembled. Desolation settled upon the house, and he wished he had left one corner of it to which he could retreat unhaunted by the child's presence. He took long tramps, avoiding the river with a sensation next to panic. It was two days before he got back to his table, and then he had made up his mind to let the boy live. To kill him off, too, was more than his augmented stock of human nature could endure. After all, the lad's death had been purely accidental, wanton. It was just that he should live – with one of the author's inimitable suggestions of future greatness; but, at the end, the parting was almost as bitter as the other. Orth knew then how men feel when their sons go forth to encounter the world and ask no more of the old companionship.

The author's boxes were packed. He sent the manuscript to his publisher an hour after it was finished – he could not have given it a final reading to have saved it from failure – directed his secretary to examine the proof under a microscope, and left the next morning for Homburg. There, in inmost circles, he forgot his children. He visited in several of the great houses of the Continent until November; then returned to London to find his book the literary topic of the day. His secretary handed him the reviews; and for once in a way he read the finalities of the nameless. He found himself hailed as a genius, and compared in astonished phrases to the prodigiously clever talent which the world for twenty years had isolated under the name of Ralph Orth. This pleased him, for every writer is human enough to wish to be hailed as a genius, and immediately. Many are, and many wait; it depends upon the fashion of the moment, and the needs and bias of those who write of writers. Orth had waited twenty years; but his past was bedecked with the headstones of geniuses long since forgotten. He was grati-fied to come thus publicly into his estate, but soon reminded himself that all the adulation of which a belated world was capable could not give him one thrill of the pleasure which the companionship of that book had given him, while creating. It was the keenest pleasure in his memory, and when a man is fifty and has written many books, that is saying a great deal.

He allowed what society was in town to lavish honours upon him for something over a month, then cancelled all his engagements and went down to Chillingsworth.

His estate was in Hertfordshire, that county of gentle hills and tangled lanes, of ancient oaks and wide wild heaths, of historic houses, and dark woods, and green fields innumerable – a Wordsworthian shire, steeped in the deepest peace of England. As Orth drove towards his own gates he had the typical English sunset to gaze upon, a red streak with a church spire against it. His woods were silent. In the fields, the cows stood as if conscious of their part. The ivy on his old grey towers had been young with his children.

He spent a haunted night, but the next day stranger happenings began.

2

He rose early, and went for one of his long walks. England seems to cry out to be walked upon, and Orth, like others of the transplanted, experienced to the full the country's gift of foot-restlessness and mental calm. Calm flees, however, when the ego is rampant, and today, as upon others too recent, Orth's soul was as restless as his feet. He had walked for two hours when he entered the wood of his neighbour's estate, a domain seldom honoured by him, as it, too, had been bought by an American – a flighty hunting widow, who displeased the fastidious taste of the author. He heard children's voices, and turned with the quick prompting of retreat.

As he did so, he came face to face, on the narrow path, with a little girl. For the moment he was possessed by the most hideous sensation which can visit a man's being – abject terror. He believed that body and soul were disintegrating. The child before him was his child, the original of a portrait in which the artist, dead two centuries ago, had missed exact fidelity, after all. The difference, even his rolling vision took note, lay in the warm pure living whiteness and the deeper spiritual suggestion of the child in his path. Fortunately for his self-respect, the surrender lasted but a moment. The little girl spoke.

'You look real sick,' she said. 'Shall I lead you home?'

The voice was soft and sweet, but the intonation, the vernacular, were American, and not of the highest class. The shock was, if possible, more agonising than the other, but this time Orth rose to the occasion.

'Who are you?' he demanded, with asperity. 'What is your name? Where do you live?'

The child smiled, an angelic smile, although she was evidently amused. 'I never had so many questions asked me all at once,' she said. 'But I don't mind, and I'm glad you're not sick. I'm Mrs Jennie Root's little girl – my father's dead. My name is Blanche – you *are* sick! No? – and I live in Rome, New York State. We've come over here to visit pa's relations.'

Orth took the child's hand in his. It was very warm and soft.

'Take me to your mother,' he said, firmly; 'now, at once. You can return and play afterwards. And as I wouldn't have you disappointed for the world, I'll send to town today for a beautiful doll.'

The little girl, whose face had fallen, flashed her delight, but walked with great dignity beside him. He groaned in his depths as he saw they were pointing for the widow's house, but made up his mind that he would know the history of the child and of all her ancestors, if he had to sit down at table with his obnoxious neighbour. To his surprise, however, the child did not lead him into the park, but towards one of the old stone houses of the tenantry.

'Pa's great-great-great-grandfather lived there,' she remarked, with all the American's pride of ancestry. Orth did not smile, however. Only the warm clasp of the hand in his, the soft thrilling voice of his still mysterious companion, prevented him from feeling as if moving through the mazes of one of his own famous ghost stories.

The child ushered him into the dining-room, where an old man was seated at the table reading his Bible. The room was at least eight hundred years old. The ceiling was supported by the trunk of a tree, black, and probably petrified. The windows had still their diamond panes, separated, no doubt, by the original lead. Beyond was a large kitchen in which were several women. The old man, who looked patriarchal enough to have laid the foundations of his dwelling, glanced up and regarded the visitor without hospitality. His expression softened as his eyes moved to the child.

'Who 'ave ye brought?' he asked. He removed his spectacles. 'Ah!' He rose, and offered the author a chair. At the same moment, the women entered the room.

'Of course you've fallen in love with Blanche, sir,' said one of them. 'Everybody does.'

'Yes, that is it. Quite so.' Confusion still prevailing among his faculties, he clung to the naked truth. 'This little girl has interested and startled me because she bears a precise resemblance to one of the portraits in Chillingsworth – painted about two hundred years ago. Such extraordinary likenesses do not occur without reason, as a rule, and, as I admired my portrait so deeply that I have written a story about it, you will not think it unnatural if I am more than curious to discover the reason for this resemblance. The little girl tells me that her ancestors lived in this very house, and as my little girl lived next door, so to speak, there undoubtedly is a natural reason for the resemblance.'

His host closed the Bible, put his spectacles in his pocket, and hobbled out of the house.

'He'll never talk of family secrets,' said an elderly woman, who introduced herself as the old man's daughter, and had placed bread and milk before the guest. 'There are secrets in every family, and we have ours, but he'll never tell those old tales. All I can tell you is that an ancestor of little Blanche went to wreck and ruin because of some fine lady's doings, and killed himself. The story is that his boys turned out bad. One of them saw his crime, and never got over the shock; he was foolish like, after. The mother was a poor scared sort of creature, and hadn't much influence over the other boy. There seemed to be a blight on all the man's descendants, until one of them went to America. Since then, they haven't prospered, exactly, but they've done better, and they don't drink so heavy.'

'They haven't done so well,' remarked a worn patient-looking woman. Orth typed her as belonging to the small middle-class of an interior town of the eastern United States.

'You are not the child's mother?'

'Yes, sir. Everybody is surprised; you needn't apologise. She doesn't look like any of us, although her brothers and sisters are good enough for anybody to be proud of. But we all think she strayed in by mistake, for she looks like any lady's child, and, of course, we're only middle-class.'

Orth gasped. It was the first time he had ever heard a native American use the term middle-class with a personal application. For the moment, he forgot the child. His analytical mind raked in the new specimen. He questioned, and learned that the woman's husband had kept a hat store in Rome, New York; that her boys were clerks, her girls in stores, or typewriting. They kept her and little Blanche – who had come after her other children were well grown – in comfort; and they were all very happy together. The boys broke out, occasionally; but, on the whole, were the best in the world, and her girls were worthy of far better than they had. All were robust, except Blanche. 'She coming so late, when I was no longer young, makes her delicate,' she remarked, with a slight blush, the signal of her chaste Americanism; 'but I guess she'll get along all right. She couldn't have better care if she was a queen's child.'

Orth, who had gratefully consumed the bread and milk, rose. 'Is that really all you can tell me?' he asked.

'That's all,' replied the daughter of the house. 'And you couldn't pry open father's mouth.'

Orth shook hands cordially with all of them, for he could be charming when he chose. He offered to escort the little girl back to her playmates in the wood, and she took prompt possession of his hand. As he was leaving, he turned suddenly to Mrs Root. 'Why did you call her Blanche?' he asked.

'She was so white and dainty, she just looked it.'

Orth took the next train for London, and from Lord Teignmouth obtained the address of the aunt who lived on the family traditions, and a cordial note of introduction to her. He then spent an hour anticipating, in a toy shop, the whims and pleasures of a child – an incident of paternity which his book-children had not inspired. He bought the finest doll, piano, French dishes, cooking apparatus, and playhouse in the shop, and signed a check for thirty pounds with a sensation of positive rapture. Then he took the train for Lancashire, where the Lady Mildred Mortlake lived in another ancestral home.

Possibly there are few imaginative writers who have not a leaning, secret or avowed, to the occult. The creative gift is in very close relationship with the Great Force behind the universe; for aught we know, may be an atom thereof. It is not strange, therefore, that the lesser and closer of the unseen forces should send their vibrations to it occasionally; or, at all events, that the imagination should incline its ear to the most mysterious and picturesque of all beliefs. Orth frankly dallied with the old dogma. He formulated no personal faith of any sort, but his creative faculty, that ego within an ego, had made more than one excursion into the invisible and brought back literary treasure.

The Lady Mildred received with sweetness and warmth the generous contributor to the family sieve, and listened with fluttering interest to all he had not told the world – she had read the book – and to the strange, Americanised sequel.

'I am all at sea,' concluded Orth. 'What had my little girl to do with the tragedy? What relation was she to the lady who drove the young man to destruction – ?'

'The closest,' interrupted Lady Mildred. 'She was herself!'

Orth stared at her. Again he had a confused sense of disintegration. Lady Mildred, gratified by the success of her bolt, proceeded less dramatically: 'Wally was up here just after I read your book, and I discovered he had given you the wrong history of the picture. Not that he knew it. It is a story we have left untold as often as possible, and I tell it to you only because you would probably become a monomaniac if I didn't. Blanche Mortlake – that Blanche, there had been several of her name, but there has not been one since – did not die in childhood, but lived to be twenty-four. She was an angelic child, but little angels sometimes grow up into very naughty girls. I believe she was delicate as a child, which probably gave her that spiritual look. Perhaps she was spoiled and flattered, until her poor little soul was stifled, which is likely. At all events, she was the coquette of her day – she seemed to care for nothing but breaking hearts; and she did not stop when she married, either. She hated her husband, and became reckless. She had no children. So far, the tale is not an uncommon one; but the worst, and what makes the ugliest stain in our annals, is to come.

'She was alone one summer at Chillingsworth – where she had taken temporary refuge from her husband – and she amused herself – some say, fell in love – with a young man of the yeomanry, a tenant of the next estate. His name was Root. He, so it comes down to us, was a magnificent specimen of his kind, and in those days the yeomanry gave us our great soldiers. His beauty of face was quite as remarkable as his physique; he led all the rural youth in sport, and was a bit above his class in every way. He had a wife in no way remarkable, and two little boys, but was always more with his friends than his family. Where he and Blanche Mortlake met I don't know – in the woods, probably, although it has been said that he had the run of the house. But, at all events, he was wild about her, and she pretended to be about him. Perhaps she was, for women have stooped before and since. Some women can be stormed by a fine man in any circumstances; but, although I am a woman of the world, and not easy to shock, there are some things I tolerate so hardly that it is all I can do to bring myself to believe in them; and stooping is one. Well, they were the scandal of the county for months, and then, either because she had tired of her new toy, or his grammar grated after the first glamour, or because she feared her husband, who was returning from the Continent, she broke off with him and returned to town. He followed her, and forced his way into her house. It is said she melted, but made him swear never to attempt to see her again.

He returned to his home, and killed himself. A few months later she took her own life. That is all I know.'

'It is quite enough for me,' said Orth.

The next night, as his train travelled over the great wastes of Lancashire, a thousand chimneys were spouting forth columns of fire. Where the sky was not red it was black. The place looked like hell. Another time Orth's imagination would have gathered immediate inspiration from this wildest region of England. The fair and peaceful counties of the south had nothing to compare in infernal grandeur with these acres of flaming columns. The chimneys were invisible in the lower darkness of the night; the fires might have leaped straight from the angry caldron of the earth.

But Orth was in a subjective world, searching for all he had ever heard of occultism. He recalled that the sinful dead are doomed, according to this belief, to linger for vast reaches of time in that borderland which is close to earth, eventually sent back to work out their final salvation; that they work it out among the descendants of the people they have wronged; that suicide is held by the devotees of occultism to be a cardinal sin, abhorred and execrated.

Authors are far closer to the truths enfolded in mystery than ordinary people, because of that very audacity of imagination which irritates their plodding critics. As only those who dare to make mistakes succeed greatly, only those who shake free the wings of their imagination brush, once in a way, the secrets of the great pale world. If such writers go wrong, it is not for the mere brains to tell them so.

Upon Orth's return to Chillingsworth, he called at once upon the child, and found her happy among his gifts. She put her arms about his neck, and covered his serene unlined face with soft kisses. This completed the conquest. Orth from that moment adored her as a child, irrespective of the psychological problem.

Gradually he managed to monopolise her. From long walks it was but a step to take her home for luncheon. The hours of her visits lengthened. He had a room fitted up as a nursery and filled with the wonders of toyland. He took her to London to see the pantomimes; two days before Christmas, to buy presents for her relatives; and together they strung them upon the most wonderful Christmas-tree that the old hall of Chillingsworth had ever embraced. She had a donkey-cart, and a trained nurse, disguised as a maid, to wait upon her. Before a month had passed she was living in state at Chillingsworth and paying daily visits to her mother. Mrs Root was deeply flattered, and apparently well content. Orth told her plainly that he should make the child independent, and educate her, meanwhile. Mrs Root intended to spend six months in England, and Orth was in no hurry to alarm her by broaching his ultimate design.

He reformed Blanche's accent and vocabulary, and read to her out of books which would have addled the brains of most little maids of six; but she seemed to enjoy them, although she seldom made a comment. He was always ready to play games with her, but she was a gentle little thing, and, moreover, tired easily. She preferred to sit in the depths of a big chair, toasting her bare toes at the log-fire in the hall, while her friend read or talked to her. Although she was thoughtful, and, when left to herself, given to dreaming, his patient observation could detect nothing uncanny about her. Moreover, she had a quick sense of humour, she was easily amused, and could laugh as merrily as any child in the world. He was resigning all hope of further development on the shadowy side when one day he took her to the picture-gallery.

It was the first warm day of summer. The gallery was not heated, and he had not dared to take his frail visitor into its chilly spaces during the winter and spring. Although he had wished to see the effect of the picture on the child, he had shrunk from the bare possibility of the very developments the mental part of him craved; the other was warmed and satisfied for the first time, and held itself aloof from disturbance. But one day the sun streamed through the old windows, and, obeying a sudden impulse, he led Blanche to the gallery.

It was some time before he approached the child of his earlier love. Again he hesitated. He pointed out many other fine pictures, and Blanche smiled appreciatively at his remarks, that were wise in criticism and interesting in matter. He never knew just how much she understood, but the very fact that there were depths in the child beyond his probing riveted his chains.

Suddenly he wheeled about and waved his hand to her prototype. 'What do you think of that?' he asked. 'You remember, I told you of the likeness the day I met you.'

She looked indifferently at the picture, but he noticed that her colour changed oddly; its pure white tone gave place to an equally delicate grey.

'I have seen it before,' she said. 'I came in here one day to look at it. And I have been quite often since. You never forbade me,' she added, looking at him appealingly, but dropping her eyes quickly. 'And I like the little girl – and the boy – very much.'

'Do you? Why?'

'I don't know' – a formula in which she had taken refuge before. Still her candid eyes were lowered; but she was quite calm. Orth, instead of questioning, merely fixed his eyes upon her, and waited. In a moment she stirred uneasily, but she did not laugh nervously, as another child would have done. He had never seen her self-possession ruffled, and he had begun to doubt he ever should. She was full of human warmth and affection. She seemed made for love, and every creature who came within her ken adored her, from the author himself down to the litter of puppies presented to her by the stable-boy a few weeks since; but her serenity would hardly be enhanced by death.

She raised her eyes finally, but not to his. She looked at the portrait.

'Did you know that there was another picture behind?' she asked.

'No,' replied Orth, turning cold. 'How did you know it?'

'One day I touched a spring in the frame, and this picture came forward. Shall I show you?'

'Yes!' And crossing curiosity and the involuntary shrinking from impending phenomena was a sensation of aesthetic disgust that *he* should be treated to a secret spring.

The little girl touched hers, and that other Blanche sprang aside so quickly that she might have been impelled by a sharp blow from behind. Orth narrowed his eyes and stared at what she revealed. He felt that his own Blanche was watching him, and set his features, although his breath was short.

There was the Lady Blanche Mortlake in the splendour of her young womanhood, beyond a doubt. Gone were all traces of her spiritual childhood, except, perhaps, in the shadows of the mouth; but more than fulfilled were the promises of her mind. Assuredly, the woman had been as brilliant and gifted as she had been restless and passionate. She wore her very pearls with arrogance, her very hands were tense with eager life, her whole being breathed mutiny.

Orth turned abruptly to Blanche, who had transferred her attention to the picture.

'What a tragedy is there!' he exclaimed, with a fierce attempt at lightness. 'Think of a woman having all that pent up within her two centuries ago! And at the mercy of a stupid family, no doubt, and a still stupider husband. No wonder – today, a woman like that might not be a model for all the virtues, but she certainly would use her gifts and become famous, the while living her life too fully to have any place in it for yeomen and such, or even for the trivial business of breaking hearts.' He put his finger under Blanche's chin, and raised her face, but he could not compel her gaze. 'You are the exact image of that little girl,' he said, 'except that you are even purer and finer. She had no chance, none whatever. You live in the woman's age. Your opportunities will be infinite. I shall see to it that they are. What you wish to be you shall be. There will be no pent-up energies here to burst out into disaster for yourself and others. You shall be trained to self-control – that is, if you ever develop self-will, dear child – every faculty shall be educated, every school of life you desire knowledge through shall be opened to you. You shall become that finest flower of civilisation, a woman who knows how to use her independence.'

She raised her eyes slowly, and gave him a look which stirred the roots of sensation – a long look of unspeakable melancholy. Her chest rose once; then she set her lips tightly, and dropped her eyes.

'What do you mean?' he cried, roughly, for his soul was chattering. 'Is – it – do you – ?' He dared not go too far, and concluded lamely, 'You mean you fear that your mother will not give you to me when she goes – you have divined that I wish to adopt you? Answer me, will you?'

But she only lowered her head and turned away, and he, fearing to frighten or repel her, apologised for his abruptness, restored the outer picture to its place, and led her from the gallery.

He sent her at once to the nursery, and when she came down to luncheon and took her place at his right hand, she was as natural and childlike as ever. For some days he restrained his curiosity, but one evening, as they were sitting before the fire in the hall listening to the storm, and just after he had told her the story of the erl-king, he took her on his knee and asked her gently if she would not tell him what had been in her thoughts when he had drawn her brilliant future. Again her face turned grey, and she dropped her eyes.

'I cannot,' she said. 'I – perhaps – I don't know.'

'Was it what I suggested?'

She shook her head, then looked at him with a shrinking appeal which forced him to drop the subject.

He went the next day alone to the gallery, and looked long at the portrait of the woman. She stirred no response in him. Nor could he feel that the woman of Blanche's future would stir the man in him. The paternal was all he had to give, but that was hers forever.

He went out into the park and found Blanche digging in her garden, very dirty and absorbed. The next afternoon, however, entering the hall noiselessly, he saw her sitting in her big chair, gazing out into nothing visible, her whole face settled in melancholy. He asked her if she were ill, and she recalled herself at once, but confessed to feeling tired. Soon after this he noticed that she lingered longer in the comfortable depths of her chair, and seldom went out, except with himself. She insisted that she was quite well, but after he had surprised her again looking as sad as if she had renounced every joy of childhood, he summoned from London a doctor renowned for his success with children.

The scientist questioned and examined her. When she had left the room he shrugged his shoulders. 'She might have been born with ten years of life in her, or she might grow up into a buxom woman,' he said. 'I confess I cannot tell. She appears to be sound enough, but I have no X-rays in my eyes, and for all I know she may be on the verge of decay. She certainly has the look of those who die young. I have never seen so spiritual a child. But I can put my finger on nothing. Keep her out-of-doors, don't give her sweets, and don't let her catch anything if you can help it.'

Orth and the child spent the long warm days of summer under the trees of the park, or driving in the quiet lanes. Guests were unbidden, and his pen was idle. All that was human in him had gone out to Blanche. He loved her, and she was a perpetual delight to him. The rest of the world received the large measure of his indifference. There was no further change in her, and apprehension slept and let him sleep. He had persuaded Mrs Root to remain in England for a year. He sent her theatre tickets every week, and placed a horse and phaeton at her disposal. She was enjoying herself and seeing less and less of Blanche. He took the child to Bournemouth for a fortnight, and again to Scotland, both of which outings benefited as much as they pleased her. She had begun to tyrannise over him amiably, and she carried herself quite royally. But she was always sweet and truthful, and these qualities, combined with that something in the depths of her mind which defied his explorations, held him captive. She was devoted to him, and cared for no other companion, although she was demonstrative to her mother when they met.

It was in the tenth month of this idyll of the lonely man and the lonely child that Mrs Root flurriedly entered the library of Chillingsworth, where Orth happened to be alone.

'Oh, sir,' she exclaimed, 'I must go home. My daughter Grace writes me – she should have done it before – that the boys are not behaving as well as they should – she didn't tell me, as I was having such a good time she just hated to worry me – Heaven knows I've had enough worry – but now I must go – I just couldn't stay – boys are an awful responsibility – girls ain't a circumstance to them, although mine are a handful sometimes.'

Orth had written about too many women to interrupt the flow. He let her talk until she paused to recuperate her forces. Then he said quietly: 'I am sorry this has come so suddenly, for it forces me to broach a subject at once which I would rather have postponed until the idea had taken possession of you by degrees – '

'I know what it is you want to say, sir,' she broke in, 'and I've reproached myself that I haven't warned you before, but I didn't like to be the one to speak first. You want Blanche – of course, I couldn't help seeing that; but I can't let her go, sir, indeed, I can't.'

'Yes,' he said, firmly, 'I want to adopt Blanche, and I hardly think you can refuse, for you must know how greatly it will be to her advantage. She is a wonderful child; you have never been blind to that; she should have every opportunity, not only of money, but of association. If I adopt her legally, I shall, of course, make her my heir, and – there is no reason why she should not grow up as great a lady as any in England.'

The poor woman turned white, and burst into tears. 'I've sat up nights and nights, struggling,' she said, when she could speak. 'That, and missing her. I couldn't stand in her light, and I let her stay. I know I oughtn't to, now – I mean, stand in her light – but, sir, she is dearer than all the others put together.'

'Then live here in England – at least, for some years longer. I will gladly relieve your children of your support, and you can see Blanche as often as you choose.'

'I can't do that, sir. After all, she is only one, and there are six others. I can't desert them. They all need me, if only to keep them together – three girls unmarried and out in the world, and three boys just a little inclined to be wild. There is another point, sir – I don't exactly know how to say it.'

'Well?' asked Orth, kindly. This American woman thought him the ideal gentleman, although the mistress of the estate on which she visited called him a boor and a snob.

'It is – well – you must know – you can imagine – that her brothers and sisters just worship Blanche. They save their dimes to buy her everything she wants – or used to want. Heaven knows what will satisfy her now, although I can't see that she's one bit spoiled. But she's just like a religion to them; they're not much on church. I'll tell you, sir, what I couldn't say to anyone else, not even to these relations who've been so kind to me – but there's wildness, just a streak, in all my children, and I believe, I know, it's Blanche that keeps them straight. My girls get bitter, sometimes; work all the week and little fun, not caring for common men and no chance to marry gentlemen; and sometimes they break out and talk dreadful; then, when they're over it, they say they'll live for Blanche – they've said it over and over, and they mean it. Every sacrifice they've made for her – and they've made many – has done them good. It isn't that Blanche ever says a word of the preachy sort, or has anything of the Sunday-school child about her, or even tries to smooth them down when they're excited. It's just herself. The only thing she ever does is sometimes to draw herself up and look scornful, and that nearly kills them. Little as she is, they're crazy about having her respect. I've grown superstitious about her. Until she came I used to get frightened, terribly, sometimes, and I believe she came for that. So – you see! I know Blanche is too fine for us and ought to have the best; but, then, they are to be considered, too. They have their rights, and they've got much more good than bad in them. I don't know! I don't know! It's kept me awake many nights.'

Orth rose abruptly. 'Perhaps you will take some further time to think it over,' he said. 'You can stay a few weeks longer – the matter cannot be so pressing as that.'

The woman rose. 'I've thought this,' she said; 'let Blanche decide. I believe she knows more than any of us. I believe that whichever way she decided would be right. I won't say anything to her, so you won't think I'm working on her feelings; and I can trust you. But she'll know.'

'Why do you think that?' asked Orth, sharply. 'There is nothing uncanny about the child. She is not yet seven years old. Why should you place such a responsibility upon her?'

'Do you think she's like other children?'

'I know nothing of other children.'

'I do, sir. I've raised six. And I've seen hundreds of others. I never was one to be a fool about my own, but Blanche isn't like any other child living – I'm certain of it.'

'What *do* you think?'

And the woman answered, according to her lights: 'I think she's an angel, and came to us because we needed her.'

'And I think she is Blanche Mortlake working out the last of her salvation,' thought the author; but he made no reply, and was alone in a moment.

It was several days before he spoke to Blanche, and then, one morning, when she was sitting on her mat on the lawn with the light full upon her, he told her abruptly that her mother must return home.

To his surprise, but unutterable delight, she burst into tears and flung herself into his arms.

'You need not leave me,' he said, when he could find his own voice. 'You can stay here always and be my little girl. It all rests with you.'

'I can't stay,' she sobbed. 'I can't!'

'And that is what made you so sad once or twice?' he asked, with a double eagerness.

She made no reply.

'Oh!' he said, passionately, 'give me your confidence, Blanche. You are the only breathing thing that I love.'

'If I could I would,' she said. 'But I don't know – not quite.'

'How much do you know?'

But she sobbed again and would not answer. He dared not risk too much. After all, the physical barrier between the past and the present was very young.

'Well, well, then, we will talk about the other matter. I will not pretend to disguise the fact that your mother is distressed at the idea of parting from you, and thinks it would be as sad for your brothers and sisters, whom she says you influence for their good. Do you think that you do?'

'Yes.'

'How do you know this?'

'Do you know why you know everything?'

'No, my dear, and I have great respect for your instincts. But your sisters and brothers are now old enough to take care of themselves. They must be of poor stuff if they cannot live properly without the aid of a child. Moreover, they will be marrying soon. That will also mean that your mother will have many little grandchildren to console her for your loss. I will be the one bereft, if you leave me. I am the only one who really needs you. I don't say I will go to the bad, as you may have very foolishly persuaded yourself your family will do without you, but I trust to your instincts to make you realise how unhappy, how inconsolable I shall be. I shall be the loneliest man on earth!'

She rubbed her face deeper into his flannels, and tightened her embrace. 'Can't you come, too?' she asked.

'No; you must live with me wholly or not at all. Your people are not my people, their ways are not my ways. We should not get along. And if you lived with me over there you might as well stay here, for your influence over them would be quite as removed. Moreover, if they are of the right stuff, the memory of you will be quite as potent for good as your actual presence.'

'Not unless I died.'

Again something within him trembled. 'Do you believe you are going to die young?' he blurted out.

But she would not answer.

He entered the nursery abruptly the next day and found her packing her dolls. When she saw him, she sat down and began to weep hopelessly. He knew then that his fate was sealed. And when, a year later, he received her last little scrawl, he was almost glad that she went when she did.

THE STRIDING PLACE

The Striding Place

Weigall, continental and detached, tired early of grouse-shooting. To stand propped against a sod fence while his host's workmen routed up the birds with long poles and drove them towards the waiting guns, made him feel himself a parody on the ancestors who had roamed the moors and forests of this West Riding of Yorkshire in hot pursuit of game worth the killing. But when in England in August he always accepted whatever proffered for the season, and invited his host to shoot pheasants on his estates in the South. The amusements of life, he argued, should be accepted with the same philosophy as its ills.

It had been a bad day. A heavy rain had made the moor so spongy that it fairly sprang beneath the feet. Whether or not the grouse had haunts of their own, wherein they were immune from rheumatism, the bag had been small. The women, too, were an unusually dull lot, with the exception of a new-minded *debutante* who bothered Weigall at dinner by demanding the verbal restoration of the vague paintings on the vaulted roof above them.

But it was no one of these things that sat on Weigall's mind as, when the other men went up to bed, he let himself out of the castle and sauntered down to the river. His intimate friend, the companion of his boyhood, the chum of his college days, his fellow-traveller in many lands, the man for whom he possessed stronger affection than for all men, had mysteriously disappeared two days ago, and his track might have sprung to the upper air for all trace he had left behind him. He had been a guest on the adjoining estate during the past week, shooting with the fervour of the true sportsman, making love in the intervals to Adeline Cavan, and apparently in the best of spirits. As far as was known there was nothing to lower his mental mercury, for his rent-roll was a large one, Miss Cavan blushed whenever he looked at her, and, being one of the best shots in England, he was never happier than in August. The suicide theory was preposterous, all agreed, and there was as little reason to believe him murdered. Nevertheless, he had walked out of March Abbey two nights ago without hat or overcoat, and had not been seen since.

The country was being patrolled night and day. A hundred keepers and workmen were beating the woods and poking the bogs on the moors, but as yet not so much as a handkerchief had been found.

Weigall did not believe for a moment that Wyatt Gifford was dead, and although it was impossible not to be affected by the general uneasiness, he was disposed to be more angry than frightened. At Cambridge Gifford had been an incorrigible practical joker, and by no means had outgrown the habit; it would be like him to cut across the country in his evening clothes, board a cattle-train, and amuse himself touching up the picture of the sensation in West Riding.

However, Weigall's affection for his friend was too deep to companion with tranquillity in the present state of doubt, and, instead of going to bed early with the other men, he determined to walk until ready for sleep. He went down to the river and followed the path through the woods. There was no moon, but the stars sprinkled their cold light upon the pretty belt of water flowing placidly past wood and ruin, between green masses of overhanging rocks or sloping banks tangled with tree and shrub, leaping occasionally over stones with the harsh notes of an angry scold, to recover its equanimity the moment the way was clear again.

It was very dark in the depths where Weigall trod. He smiled as he recalled a remark of Gifford's: 'An English wood is like a good many other things in life – very promising at a distance, but a hollow mockery when you get within. You see daylight on both sides, and the sun freckles the very bracken. Our woods need the night to make them seem what they ought to be – what they once were, before our ancestors' descendants demanded so much more money, in these so much more various days.'

Weigall strolled along, smoking, and thinking of his friend, his pranks – many of which had done more credit to his imagination than this – and recalling conversations that had lasted the night through. Just before the end of the London season they had walked the streets one hot night after a party, discussing the various theories of the soul's destiny. That afternoon they had met at the coffin of a college friend whose mind had been a blank for the past three years. Some months previously they had called at the asylum to see him. His expression had been senile, his face imprinted with the record of debauchery. In death the face was placid, intelligent, without ignoble lineation – the face of the man they had known at college. Weigall and Gifford had had no time to comment there, and the afternoon and evening were full; but, coming forth from the house of festivity together, they had reverted almost at once to the topic.

'I cherish the theory,' Gifford had said, 'that the soul sometimes lingers in the body after death. During madness, of course, it is an impotent prisoner, albeit a conscious one. Fancy its agony, and its horror! What more natural than that, when the life-spark goes out, the tortured soul should take possession of the vacant skull and triumph once more for a few hours while old friends look their last? It has had time to repent while compelled to crouch and behold the result of its work, and it has shrived itself into a state of comparative purity. If I had my way, I should stay inside my bones until the coffin had gone into its niche, that I might obviate for my poor old comrade the tragic impersonality of death. And I should like to see justice done to it, as it were – to see it lowered among its ancestors with the ceremony and solemnity that are its due. I am afraid that if I dissevered myself too quickly, I should yield to curiosity and hasten to investigate the mysteries of space.'

'You believe in the soul as an independent entity, then – that it and the vital principle are not one and the same?'

'Absolutely. The body and soul are twins, life comrades – sometimes friends, sometimes enemies, but always loyal in the last instance. Some day, when I am tired of the world, I shall go to India and become a mahatma, solely for the pleasure of receiving proof during life of this independent relationship.'

'Suppose you were not sealed up properly, and returned after one of your astral flights to find your earthly part unfit for habitation? It is an experiment I don't think I should care to try, unless even juggling with soul and flesh had palled.'

'That would not be an uninteresting predicament. I should rather enjoy experimenting with broken machinery.'

The high wild roar of water smote suddenly upon Weigall's ear and checked his memories. He left the wood and walked out on the huge slippery stones which nearly close the River Wharfe at this point, and watched the waters boil down into the narrow pass with their furious untiring energy. The black quiet of the woods rose high on either side. The stars seemed colder and whiter just above. On either hand the perspective of the river might have run into a rayless cavern. There was no lonelier spot in England, nor one which had the right to claim so many ghosts, if ghosts there were.

Weigall was not a coward, but he recalled uncomfortably the tales of those that had been done to death in the Strid.* Wordsworth's Boy of Egremond had been disposed of by the practical Whitaker; but countless others, more venturesome than wise, had gone down into that narrow boiling course, never to appear in the still pool a few yards beyond. Below the great rocks which form the walls of the Strid was believed to be a natural vault, on to whose shelves the dead were drawn. The spot had an ugly fascination. Weigall stood, visioning skeletons, uncoffined and green, the home of the eyeless things which had devoured all that had covered and filled that rattling symbol of man's mortality; then fell to wondering if anyone had attempted to leap the Strid of late. It was covered with slime; he had never seen it look so treacherous.

He shuddered and turned away, impelled, despite his manhood, to flee the spot. As he did so, something tossing in the foam below the fall – something as white, yet independent of it – caught his eye and arrested his step. Then he saw that it was describing a contrary motion to the rushing water – an upward backward motion. Weigall stood rigid, breathless; he fancied he heard the crackling of his hair. Was that a hand? It thrust itself still higher above the boiling foam, turned sidewise, and four frantic fingers were distinctly visible against the black rock beyond.

Weigall's superstitious terror left him. A man was there, struggling to free himself from the suction beneath the Strid, swept down, doubtless, but a moment before his arrival, perhaps as he stood with his back to the current.

He stepped as close to the edge as he dared. The hand doubled as if in imprecation, shaking savagely in the face of that force which leaves its creatures to immutable law; then spread wide again, clutching, expanding, crying for help as audibly as the human voice.

Weigall dashed to the nearest tree, dragged and twisted off a branch with his strong arms, and returned as swiftly to the Strid. The hand was in the same place, still gesticulating as wildly; the body was undoubtedly caught in the rocks below, perhaps already halfway along one of those hideous shelves. Weigall let himself down upon a lower rock, braced his shoulder against the mass beside him, then, leaning out over the water, thrust the branch into the hand. The

*   This striding place is called the 'Strid',
     A name which it took of yore;
     A thousand years hath it borne the name,
     And it shall a thousand more.

fingers clutched it convulsively. Weigall tugged powerfully, his own feet dragged perilously near the edge. For a moment he produced no impression, then an arm shot above the waters.

The blood sprang to Weigall's head; he was choked with the impression that the Strid had him in her roaring hold, and he saw nothing. Then the mist cleared. The hand and arm were nearer, although the rest of the body was still concealed by the foam. Weigall peered out with distended eyes. The meagre light revealed in the cuffs links of a peculiar device. The fingers clutching the branch were as familiar.

Weigall forgot the slippery stones, the terrible death if he stepped too far. He pulled with passionate will and muscle. Memories flung themselves into the hot light of his brain, trooping rapidly upon each other's heels, as in the thought of the drowning. Most of the pleasures of his life, good and bad, were identified in some way with this friend. Scenes of college days, of travel, where they had deliberately sought adventure and stood between one another and death upon more occasions than one, of hours of delightful companionship among the treasures of art, and others in the pursuit of pleasure, flashed like the changing particles of a kaleidoscope. Weigall had loved several women; but he would have flouted in these moments the thought that he had ever loved any woman as he loved Wyatt Gifford. There were so many charming women in the world, and in the thirty-two years of his life he had never known another man to whom he had cared to give his intimate friendship.

He threw himself on his face. His wrists were cracking, the skin was torn from his hands. The fingers still gripped the stick. There was life in them yet.

Suddenly something gave way. The hand swung about, tearing the branch from Weigall's grasp. The body had been liberated and flung outward, though still submerged by the foam and spray.

Weigall scrambled to his feet and sprang along the rocks, knowing that the danger from suction was over and that Gifford must be carried straight to the quiet pool. Gifford was a fish in the water and could live under it longer than most men. If he survived this, it would not be the first time that his pluck and science had saved him from drowning.

Weigall reached the pool. A man in his evening clothes floated on it, his face turned towards a projecting rock over which his arm had fallen, upholding the body. The hand that had held the branch hung limply over the rock, its white reflection visible in the black water.

Weigall plunged into the shallow pool, lifted Gifford in his arms and returned to the bank. He laid the body down and threw off his coat that he might be the freer to practise the methods of resuscitation. He was glad of the moment's respite. The valiant life in the man might have been exhausted in that last struggle. He had not dared to look at his face, to put his ear to the heart. The hesitation lasted but a moment. There was no time to lose.

He turned to his prostrate friend. As he did so, something strange and disagreeable smote his senses. For a half-moment he did not appreciate its nature. Then his teeth clacked together, his feet, his outstretched arms pointed towards the woods. But he sprang to the side of the man and bent down and peered into his face. There was no face.

THE DEAD AND THE COUNTESS

The Dead and the Countess

It was an old cemetery, and they had been long dead. Those who died nowadays were put in the new burying-place on the hill, close to the Bois d'Amour and within sound of the bells that called the living to mass. But the little church where the mass was celebrated stood faithfully beside the older dead; a new church, indeed, had not been built in that forgotten corner of Finisterre for centuries, not since the calvary on its pile of stones had been raised in the tiny square, surrounded, then as now perhaps, by grey naked cottages; not since the castle with its round tower, down on the river, had been erected for the Counts of Croisac. But the stone walls enclosing that ancient cemetery had been kept in good repair, and there were no weeds within, nor toppling headstones. It looked cold and grey and desolate, like all the cemeteries of Brittany, but it was made hideous neither by tawdry gewgaws nor the licence of time.

And sometimes it was close to a picture of beauty. When the village celebrated its yearly *pardon*, a great procession came out of the church – priests in glittering robes, young men in their gala costume of black and silver, holding flashing standards aloft, and many maidens in flapping white head-dress and collar, black frocks and aprons flaunting with ribbons and lace. They marched, chanting, down the road beside the wall of the cemetery, where lay the generations that in their day had held the banners and chanted the service of the *pardon*. For the dead were peasants and priests – the Croisacs had their burying-place in a hollow of the hills behind the castle – old men and women who had wept and died for the fishermen that had gone to the *grande pêche* and returned no more, and now and again a child slept there. Those who walked past the dead at the *pardon*, or after the marriage ceremony, or took part in any one of the minor religious festivals with which the Catholic village enlivens its existence – all, young and old, looked grave and sad. For the women from childhood know that their lot is to wait and dread and weep, and the men that the ocean is treacherous and cruel, but that bread can be wrung from no other master. Therefore the living have little sympathy for the dead who have laid down their crushing burden; and the dead under their stones slumber contentedly enough. There is no envy among them for the young who wander at evening and pledge their troth in the Bois d'Amour, only pity for the groups of women who wash their linen in the creek that flows to the river. They look like pictures in the green quiet book of nature, these women, in their glistening white head-gear and deep collars; but the dead know better than to envy them, and the women – and the lovers – know better than to pity the dead.

The dead lay at rest in their boxes and thanked God they were quiet and had found everlasting peace.

And one day even this, for which they had patiently endured life, was taken from them.

The village was picturesque and there was none quite like it, even in Finisterre. Artists discovered it and made it famous. After the artists followed the tourists, and the old creaking *diligence* became an absurdity. Brittany was the fashion for three months of the year, and wherever there is fashion there is at least one railway. The one built to satisfy the thousands who wished to visit the wild, sad beauties of the west of France was laid along the road beside the little cemetery of this tale.

It takes a long while to awaken the dead. These heard neither the voluble working-men nor even the first snort of the engine. And, of course, they neither heard nor knew of the pleadings of the old priest that the line should be laid elsewhere. One night he came out into the old cemetery and sat on a grave and wept. For he loved his dead and felt it to be a tragic pity that the greed of money, and the fever of travel, and the petty ambitions of men whose place was in the great cities where such ambitions were born, should shatter forever the holy calm of those who had suffered so much on earth. He had known many of them in life, for he was very old; and although he believed, like all good Catholics, in heaven and purgatory and hell, yet he always saw his friends as he had buried them, peacefully asleep in their coffins, the souls lying with folded hands like the bodies that held them, patiently awaiting the final call. He would never have told you, this good old priest, that he believed heaven to be a great echoing palace in which God and the archangels dwelt alone waiting for that great day when the elected dead should rise and enter the Presence together, for he was a simple old man who had read and thought little; but he had a zigzag of fancy in his humble mind, and he saw his friends and his ancestors' friends as I have related to you, soul and body in the deep undreaming sleep of death, but sleep, not a rotted body deserted by its affrighted mate; and to all who sleep there comes, sooner or later, the time of awakening.

He knew that they had slept through the wild storms that rage on the coast of Finisterre, when ships are flung on the rocks and trees crash down in the Bois d'Amour. He knew that the soft, slow chantings of the *pardon* never struck a chord in those frozen memories, meagre and monotonous as their store had been; nor the bagpipes down in the open village hall – a mere roof on poles – when the bride and her friends danced for three days without a smile on their sad brown faces.

All this the dead had known in life and it could not disturb nor interest them now. But that hideous intruder from modern civilisation, a train of cars with a screeching engine, that would shake the earth which held them and rend the peaceful air with such discordant sounds that neither dead nor living could sleep! His life had been one long unbroken sacrifice, and he sought in vain to imagine one greater, which he would cheerfully assume could this disaster be spared his dead.

But the railway was built, and the first night the train went screaming by, shaking the earth and rattling the windows of the church, he went out and sprinkled every grave with holy water.

And thereafter, twice a day, at dawn and at night, as the train tore a noisy tunnel in the quiet air, like the plebeian upstart it was, he sprinkled every grave, rising sometimes from a bed of pain, at other times defying wind and rain and hail. And for a while he believed that his holy device had deepened the sleep of his dead, locked them beyond the power of man to awake. But one night he heard them muttering.

It was late. There were but a few stars on a black sky. Not a breath of wind came over the lonely plains beyond, or from the sea. There would be no wrecks tonight, and all the world seemed at peace. The lights were out in the village. One burned in the tower of Croisac, where the young wife of the count lay ill. The priest had been with her when the train thundered by, and she had whispered to him: 'Would that I were on it! Oh, this lonely, lonely land! this cold echoing château, with no-one to speak to day after day! If it kills me, *mon père*, make him lay me in the cemetery by the road, that twice a day I may hear the train go by – the train that goes to Paris!

If they put me down there over the hill, I will shriek in my coffin every night.'

The priest had ministered as best he could to the ailing soul of the young noblewoman, with whose like he seldom dealt, and hastened back to his dead. He mused, as he toiled along the dark road with rheumatic legs, on the fact that the woman should have the same fancy as himself.

'If she is really sincere, poor young thing,' he thought aloud, 'I will forbear to sprinkle holy water on her grave. For those who suffer while alive should have all they desire after death, and I am afraid the count neglects her. But I pray God that my dead have not heard that monster tonight.' And he tucked his gown under his arm and hurriedly told his rosary.

But when he went about among the graves with the holy water he heard the dead muttering.

'Jean-Marie,' said a voice, fumbling among its unused tones for forgotten notes, 'art thou ready? Surely that is the last call.'

'Nay, nay,' rumbled another voice, 'that is not the sound of a trumpet, Francois. That will be sudden and loud and sharp, like the great blasts of the north when they come plunging over the sea from out the awful gorges of Iceland. Dost thou remember them, Francois? Thank the good God they spared us to die in our beds with our grandchildren about us and only the little wind sighing in the Bois d'Amour. Ah, the poor comrades that died in their manhood, that went to the grande pêche once too often! Dost thou remember when the great wave curled round Ignace like his poor wife's arms, and we saw him no more? We clasped each other's hands, for we believed that we should follow, but we lived and went again and again to the *grande pêche*, and died in our beds. *Grâce à Dieu!*'

'Why dost thou think of that now – here in the grave where it matters not, even to the living?'

'I know not; but it was of that night when Ignace went down that I thought as the living breath went out of me. Of what didst thou think as thou layest dying?'

'Of the money I owed to Dominique and could not pay. I sought to ask my son to pay it, but death had come suddenly and I could not speak. God knows how they treat my name today in the village of St Hilaire.'

'Thou art forgotten,' murmured another voice. 'I died forty years after thee and men remember not so long in Finisterre. But thy son was my friend and I remember that he paid the money.'

'And my son, what of him? Is he, too, here?'

'Nay; he lies deep in the northern sea. It was his second voyage, and he had returned with a purse for the young wife, the first time. But he returned no more, and she washed in the river for the dames of Croisac, and by-and-by she died. I would have married her, but she said it was enough to lose one husband. I married another, and she grew ten years in every three that I went to the *grande pêche*. Alas for Brittany, she has no youth!'

'And thou? Wert thou an old man when thou camest here?'

'Sixty. My wife came first, like many wives. She lies here. Jeanne!'

'Is't thy voice, my husband? Not the Lord Jesus Christ's? What miracle is this? I thought that terrible sound was the trump of doom.'

'It could not be, old Jeanne, for we are still in our graves. When the trump sounds we shall have wings and robes of light, and fly straight up to heaven. Hast thou slept well?'

'Ay! But why are we awakened? Is it time for purgatory? Or have we been there?'

'The good God knows. I remember nothing. Art frightened? Would that I could hold thy hand, as when thou didst slip from life into that long sleep thou didst fear, yet welcome.'

'I am frightened, my husband. But it is sweet to hear thy voice, hoarse and hollow as it is from the mould of the grave. Thank the good God thou didst bury me with the rosary in my hands,' and she began telling the beads rapidly.

'If God is good,' cried Francois, harshly, and his voice came plainly to the priest's ears, as if the lid of the coffin had rotted, 'why are we awakened before our time? What foul fiend was it that thundered and screamed through the frozen avenues of my brain? Has God, perchance, been vanquished and does the Evil One reign in His stead?'

'Tut, tut! Thou blasphemest! God reigns, now and always. It is but a punishment He has laid upon us for the sins of earth.'

'Truly, we were punished enough before we descended to the peace of this narrow house. Ah, but it is dark and cold! Shall we lie like this for an eternity, perhaps? On earth we longed for death, but feared the grave. I would that I were alive again, poor and old and alone and in pain. It were better than this. Curse the foul fiend that woke us!'

'Curse not, my son,' said a soft voice, and the priest stood up and uncovered and crossed himself, for it was the voice of his aged predecessor. 'I cannot tell thee what this is that has rudely shaken us in our graves and freed our spirits of their blessed thraldom, and I like not the consciousness of this narrow house, this load of earth on my tired heart. But it is right, it must be right, or it would not be at all – ah, me!'

For a baby cried softly, hopelessly, and from a grave beyond came a mother's anguished attempt to still it.

'Ah, the good God!' she cried. 'I, too, thought it was the great call, and that in a moment I should rise and find my child and go to my Ignace, my Ignace whose bones lie white on the floor of the sea. Will he find them, my father, when the dead shall rise again? To lie here and doubt! – that were worse than life.'

'Yes, yes,' said the priest; 'all will be well, my daughter.'

'But all is not well, my father, for my baby cries and is alone in a little box in the ground. If I could claw my way to her with my hands – but my old mother lies between us.'

'Tell your beads!' commanded the priest, sternly – 'tell your beads, all of you. All ye that have not your beads, say the "Hail Mary!" one hundred times.'

Immediately a rapid, monotonous muttering arose from every lonely chamber of that desecrated ground. All obeyed but the baby, who still moaned with the hopeless grief of deserted children. The living priest knew that they would talk no more that night, and went into the church to pray till dawn. He was sick with horror and terror, but not for himself. When the sky was pink and the air full of the sweet scents of morning, and a piercing scream tore a rent in the early silences, he hastened out and sprinkled his graves with a double allowance of holy water. The train rattled by with two short derisive shrieks, and before the earth had ceased to tremble the priest laid his ear to the ground. Alas, they were still awake!

'The fiend is on the wing again,' said Jean-Marie; 'but as he passed I felt as if the finger of God touched my brow. It can do us no harm.'

'I, too, felt that heavenly caress!' exclaimed the old priest. 'And I!' 'And I!' 'And I!' came from every grave but the baby's.

The priest of earth, deeply thankful that his simple device had comforted them, went rapidly down the road to the castle. He forgot that he had not broken his fast nor slept. The count was one of the directors of the railroad, and to him he would make a final appeal.

It was early, but no-one slept at Croisac. The young countess was dead. A great bishop had arrived in the night and administered extreme unction. The priest hopefully asked if he might venture into the presence of the bishop. After a long wait in the kitchen, he was told that he could speak with *Monsieur l'Evèque*. He followed the servant up the wide spiral stair of the tower, and from its twenty-eighth step entered a room hung with purple cloth stamped with golden fleurs-de-lis. The bishop lay six feet above the floor on one of the splendid carved cabinet beds that are built against the walls in Brittany. Heavy curtains shaded his cold white face. The priest, who was small and bowed, felt immeasurably below that august presence, and sought for words.

'What is it, my son?' asked the bishop, in his cold weary voice. 'Is the matter so pressing? I am very tired.'

Brokenly, nervously, the priest told his story, and as he strove to convey the tragedy of the tormented dead he not only felt the poverty of his expression – for he was little used to narrative – but the torturing thought assailed him that what he said sounded wild and unnatural, real as it was to him. But he was not prepared for its effect on the bishop. He was standing in the middle of the room, whose gloom was softened and gilded by the waxen lights of a huge candelabra; his eyes, which had wandered unseeingly from one massive piece of carved furniture to another, suddenly lit on the bed, and he stopped abruptly, his tongue rolling out. The bishop was sitting up, livid with wrath.

'And this was thy matter of life and death, thou prating madman!' he thundered. 'For this string of foolish lies I am kept from my rest, as if I were another old lunatic like thyself! Thou art not fit to be a priest and have the care of souls. Tomorrow – '

But the priest had fled, wringing his hands.

As he stumbled down the winding stair he ran straight into the arms of the count. Monsieur de Croisac had just closed a door behind him. He opened it, and, leading the priest into the room, pointed to his dead countess, who lay high up against the wall, her hands clasped, unmindful for evermore of the six feet of carved cupids and lilies that upheld her. On high pedestals at head and foot of her magnificent couch the pale flames rose from tarnished golden candlesticks. The blue hangings of the room, with their white fleurs-de-lis, were faded, like the rugs on the old dim floor; for the splendour of the Croisacs had departed with the Bourbons. The count lived in the old château because he must; but he reflected bitterly tonight that if he had made the mistake of bringing a young girl to it, there were several things he might have done to save her from despair and death.

'Pray for her,' he said to the priest. 'And you will bury her in the old cemetery. It was her last request.'

He went out, and the priest sank on his knees and mumbled his prayers for the dead. But his eyes wandered to the high narrow windows through which the countess had stared for hours and days, stared at the fishermen sailing north for the *grande pêche*, followed along the shore of the river by wives and mothers, until their boats were caught in the great waves of the ocean beyond; often at naught more animate than the dark flood, the wooded banks, the ruins, the rain driving like needles through the water. The priest had eaten nothing since his meagre breakfast at twelve the day before, and his imagination was active. He wondered if the soul up there rejoiced in the death of the beautiful restless body, the passionate brooding mind. He could not see her face from where he knelt, only the waxen hands clasping a crucifix. He wondered if the face were peaceful in death, or peevish and angry as when he had seen it last. If the great change had smoothed and sealed it, then perhaps the soul would sink deep under the dark waters, grateful for oblivion, and that cursed train could not awaken it for years to come. Curiosity succeeded wonder. He cut his prayers short, got to his weary swollen feet and pushed a chair to the bed. He mounted it and his face was close to the dead woman's. Alas! it was not peaceful. It was stamped with the tragedy of a bitter renunciation. After all, she had been young, and at the last had died unwillingly. There was still a fierce tenseness about the nostrils, and her upper lip was curled as if her last word had been an imprecation. But she was very beautiful, despite the emaciation of her features. Her black hair nearly covered the bed, and her lashes looked too heavy for the sunken cheeks.

'*Pauvre petite!*' thought the priest. 'No, she will not rest, nor would she wish to. I will not sprinkle holy water on her grave. It is wondrous that monster can give comfort to anyone, but if he can, so be it.'

He went into the little oratory adjoining the bedroom and prayed more fervently. But when the watchers came an hour later they found him in a stupor, huddled at the foot of the altar.

When he awoke he was in his own bed in his little house beside the church. But it was four days before they would let him rise to go about his duties, and by that time the countess was in her grave.

The old housekeeper left him to take care of himself. He waited eagerly for the night. It was raining thinly, a grey quiet rain that blurred the landscape and soaked the ground in the Bois d'Amour. It was wet about the graves, too; but the priest had given little heed to the elements in his long life of crucified self, and as he heard the remote echo of the evening train he hastened out with his holy water and had sprinkled every grave but one when the train sped by.

Then he knelt and listened eagerly. It was five days since he had knelt there last. Perhaps they had sunk again to rest. In a moment he wrung his hands and raised them to heaven. All the earth beneath him was filled with lamentation. They wailed for mercy, for peace, for rest; they cursed the foul fiend who had shattered the locks of death; and among the voices of men and children the priest distinguished the quavering notes of his aged predecessor; not cursing, but praying with bitter entreaty. The baby was screaming with the accents of mortal terror and its mother was too frantic to care.

'Alas,' cried the voice of Jean-Marie, 'that they never told us what purgatory was like! What do the priests know? When we were threatened with punishment of our sins not a hint did we have of this. To sleep for a few hours, haunted with the moment of awakening! Then a cruel insult from the earth that is tired of us, and the orchestra of hell. Again! and again! and again! Oh God! How long? How long?'

The priest stumbled to his feet and ran over graves and paths to the mound above the countess. There he would hear a voice praising the monster of night and dawn, a note of content in this terrible chorus of despair which he believed would drive him mad. He vowed that on the morrow he would move his dead, if he had to un-bury them with his own hands and carry them up the hill to graves of his own making.

For a moment he heard no sound. He knelt and laid his ear to the grave, then pressed it more closely and held his breath. A long rumbling moan reached it, then another and another. But there were no words.

'Is she moaning in sympathy with my poor friends?' he thought; 'or have they terrified her? Why does she not speak to them? Perhaps they would forget their plight were she to tell them of the world they have left so long. But it was not their world. Perhaps that it is which distresses her, for she will be lonelier here than on earth. Ah!'

A sharp horrified cry pierced to his ears, then a gasping shriek, and another; all dying away in a dreadful smothered rumble.

The priest rose and wrung his hands, looking to the wet skies for inspiration.

'Alas!' he sobbed, 'she is not content. She has made a terrible mistake. She would rest in the deep sweet peace of death, and that monster of iron and fire and the frantic dead about her are tormenting a soul so tormented in life. There may be rest for her in the vault behind the castle, but not here. I know, and I shall do my duty – now, at once.'

He gathered his robes about him and ran as fast as his old legs and rheumatic feet would take him towards the château, whose lights gleamed through the rain. On the bank of the river he met a fisherman and begged to be taken by boat. The fisherman wondered, but picked the priest up in his strong arms, lowered him into the boat, and rowed swiftly towards the château. When they landed he made fast.

'I will wait for you in the kitchen, my father,' he said; and the priest blessed him and hurried up to the castle.

Once more he entered through the door of the great kitchen, with its blue tiles, its glittering brass and bronze warming-pans which had comforted nobles and monarchs in the days of Croisac splendour. He sank into a chair beside the stove while a maid hastened to the count. She returned while the priest was still shivering, and announced that her master would see his holy visitor in the library.

It was a dreary room where the count sat waiting for the priest, and it smelled of musty calf, for the books on the shelves were old. A few novels and newspapers lay on the heavy table, a fire burned on the andirons, but the paper on the wall was very dark and the fleurs-de-lis were tarnished and dull. The count, when at home, divided his time between this library and the water, when he could not chase the boar or the stag in the forests. But he often went to Paris, where he could afford the life of a bachelor in a wing of his great hôtel; he had known too much of the extravagance of women to give his wife the key of the faded salons. He had loved the beautiful girl when he married her, but her repinings and bitter discontent had alienated him, and during the past year he had held himself aloof from her in sullen resentment. Too late he understood, and dreamed passionately of atonement. She had been a high-spirited brilliant eager creature, and her unsatisfied mind had dwelt constantly on the world she had vividly enjoyed for one year. And he had given her so little in return!

He rose as the priest entered, and bowed low. The visit bored him, but the good old priest commanded his respect; moreover, he had performed many offices and rites in his family. He moved a chair towards his guest, but the old man shook his head and nervously twisted his hands together.

'Alas, *monsieur le comte*,' he said, 'it may be that you, too, will tell me that I am an old lunatic, as did *Monsieur l'Evèque*. Yet I must speak, even if you tell your servants to fling me out of the chateau.'

The count had started slightly. He recalled certain acid comments of the bishop, followed by a statement that a young *curé* should be sent, gently to supersede the old priest, who was in his dotage. But he replied suavely: 'You know, my father, that no-one in this castle will ever show you disrespect. Say what you wish; have no fear. But will you not sit down? I am very tired.'

The priest took the chair and fixed his eyes appealingly on the count.

'It is this, monsieur.' He spoke rapidly, lest his courage should go. 'That terrible train, with its brute of iron and live coals and foul smoke and screeching throat, has awakened my dead. I guarded them with holy water and they heard it not, until one night when I missed – I was with madame as the train shrieked by shaking the nails out of the coffins. I hurried back, but the mischief was done, the dead were awake, the dear sleep of eternity was shattered. They thought it was the last trump and wondered why they still were in their graves. But they talked together and it was not so bad at the first. But now they are frantic. They are in hell, and I have come to beseech you to see that they are moved far up on the hill. Ah, think, think, monsieur, what it is to have the last long sleep of the grave so rudely disturbed – the sleep for which we live and endure so patiently!'

He stopped abruptly and caught his breath. The count had listened without change of countenance, convinced that he was facing a madman. But the farce wearied him, and involuntarily his hand had moved towards a bell on the table.

'Ah, monsieur, not yet! not yet!' panted the priest. 'It is of the countess I came to speak. I had forgotten. She told me she wished to lie there and listen to the train go by to Paris, so I sprinkled no holy water on her grave. But she, too, is wretched and horror-stricken, monsieur. She moans and screams. Her coffin is new and strong, and I cannot hear her words, but I have heard those frightful sounds from her grave tonight, monsieur; I swear it on the cross. Ah, monsieur, thou dost believe me at last!'

For the count, as white as the woman had been in her coffin, and shaking from head to foot, had staggered from his chair and was staring at the priest as if he saw the ghost of his countess.

'You heard – ?' he gasped.

'She is not at peace, monsieur. She moans and shrieks in a terrible, smothered way, as if a hand were on her mouth – '

But he had uttered the last of his words. The count had suddenly recovered himself and dashed from the room. The priest passed his hand across his forehead and sank slowly to the floor.

'He will see that I spoke the truth,' he thought, as he fell asleep, 'and tomorrow he will intercede for my poor friends.'

* * *

The priest lies high on the hill where no train will ever disturb him, and his old comrades of the violated cemetery are close about him. For the Count and Countess of Croisac, who adore his memory, hastened to give him in death what he most had desired in the last of his life. And with them all things are well, for a man, too, may be born again, and without descending into the grave.

THE GREATEST GOOD
OF THE GREATEST NUMBER

The Greatest Good of the Greatest Number

Morton Blaine returned to New York from his brief vacation to find awaiting him a frantic note from John Schuyler, the man nearer to him than any save himself, imploring him to 'come at once'. The appeal was supplemented with the usual intimation that the service was to be rendered to God rather than to man.

The note was twenty-four hours old. Blaine, without changing his travelling clothes, rang for a cab and was driven rapidly up the Avenue. He was a man of science, not of enthusiasms, cold, unerring, brilliant; a superb intellectual machine, which never showed a fleck of rust, unremittingly polished, and enlarged with every improvement. But for one man he cherished an abiding sympathy; to that man he hastened on the slightest summons, as he hastened now. They had been intimate in boyhood; then in later years through mutual respect for each other's high abilities and ambitions.

As the cab rolled over the asphalt of the Avenue, Blaine glanced idly at the stream of carriages returning from the Park, lifting his hat to many of the languid pretty women. He owed his minor fame to his guardianship of fashionable nerves. He could calm hysteria with a pressure of his cool flexible hand or a sudden modulation of his harsh voice. And women dreaded his wrath. There were those who averred that his eyes could smoke.

He leaned forward and raised his hat with sudden interest. She who returned his bow was as cold in her colouring as a winter night, but possessed a strength of line and depth of eye which suggested to the analyst her power to give the world a shock did Circumstance cease to run abreast of her. She was leaning back indolently in the open carriage, the sun slanting into her luminous skin and eyes, her face locked for the benefit of the chance observer, although she conversed with the faded individual at her side. As her eyes met those of the doctor her mouth convulsed suddenly, and a glance of mutual understanding passed between them. Then she raised her head with a defiant, almost reckless movement.

Blaine reached his friend's house in a moment. The man who had summoned him was walking aimlessly up and down his library. He was unshaven; his hair and his clothing were disordered. His face had the modern beauty of strength and intellect and passion and weakness. A flash of relief illuminated it as Blaine entered.

'She has been terrible!' he said. 'Terrible! I have not had the courage to call in anyone else, and I am worn out. She is asleep now, and I got out of the room for half an hour. The nurse is exhausted too. Do stay tonight.'

'I will stay. Let us go upstairs.'

As they reached the second landing two handsome children romped across the hall and flung themselves upon their father.

'Where have you been?' they demanded. 'Why do you shut yourself up on the third floor with mamma all the time? When will she get well?'

Schuyler kissed them and bade them return to the nursery.

'How long can I keep it from them?' he asked bitterly. 'What an atmosphere for children – my children! – to grow up in!'

'If you would do as I wish, and send her where she belongs – '

'I shall not. She is my wife. Moreover, concealment would then be impossible.'

They had reached the third floor. He inserted a key in a door, hesitated a moment, then said abruptly: 'I saw in a paper that *she* had returned. Can it be possible?'

'I saw her on the Avenue a few moments ago.'

Was it the doctor's imagination, or did the goaded man at his side flash him a glance of appeal?

They entered a room whose doors and windows were muffled. The furniture was solid, too solid to be moved except by muscular arms. There were no mirrors nor breakable articles of any sort.

On the bed lay a woman with ragged hair and sunken yellow face, but even in her ruin indefinably elegant. Her parted lips were black and blistered within; her shapely skinny hands clutched the quilt with the tenacious suggestion of the eagle – that long-lived defiant bird. At the bedside sat a vigorous woman, the pallor of fatigue on her face.

The creature on the bed opened her eyes. They had once been what are vaguely known as fine eyes; now they looked like blots of ink on parchment.

'Give me a drink,' she said feverishly. 'Water! water! water!' She panted, and her tongue protruded slightly. Her husband turned away, his shoulders twitching. The nurse held a silver goblet to the woman's lips. She drank greedily, then scowled up at the doctor.

'You missed it,' she said. 'I should be glad, for I hate you, only you give me more relief than they. They are afraid. They tried to fool me, the idiots! But they didn't try it twice. I bit.'

She laughed and threw her arms above her head. The loose sleeves of her gown fell back and disclosed arms speckled as if from an explosion of gunpowder.

'Just an ordinary morphine fiend,' thought the doctor. 'And she is the wife of John Schuyler!'

An hour after dinner he told the husband and nurse to go to bed. For a while he read, the woman sleeping profoundly. The house was absolutely still, or seemed to be. Had pandemonium reigned he could hardly have heard an echo of it from this isolated room. The window was open, but looked upon roofs and back yards; no sound of carriage wheels rose to break the quiet. Despite the stillness, the doctor had to strain his ear to catch the irregular breathing of the sick woman. He had a singular feeling, although the most unimaginative of men, that this third floor, containing only himself and the woman, had been sliced from the rest of the house and hung suspended in space, independent of natural laws. It was after the book had ceased to interest him that the idea shaped itself, born of another, as yet unacknowledged, skulking in the recesses of his brain. At length he laid aside the book, and going to the bed, looked down upon the woman, coldly, reflectively – exactly as he had often watched the quivering of an animal – dissected alive in the cause of science.

Studying this man's face, it was impossible to imagine it agitated by any passion except thirst for knowledge. The skin was as white as marble; the profile was straight and mathematical, the mouth a straight line, the chin as square as that of a chiselled Fate. The jaw was prominent, powerful, relentless. The eyes were deeply set and grey as polished steel. The large brow was luminous, very full – an index to the terrible intellect of the man.

As he looked down on the woman his thin nostrils twitched once and his lips compressed more firmly. Then he smiled. It was an odd, almost demoniacal smile.

'A physician,' he said, half aloud, 'has almost as much power as God. The idea strikes me that we are the personification of that useful symbol.'

He plunged his hands into his pockets, and walked up and down the long thickly carpeted room.

'These are the facts in the case,' he continued. 'The one man I love and unequivocally respect is tied, hand and foot, to that unsexed dehumanised morphine receptacle on the bed. She is hopeles. Every known specific has failed, *must* fail, for she loves the vice. He has one of the best brains of this day prolific in brains; a distressing capacity for affection, human to the core. At the age of forty-two, in the maturity of his mental powers, he carries with him a constant sickening sense of humiliation; a proud man, he lives in daily fear of exposure and shame. At the age of forty-two, in the maturity of his manhood, he meets the woman who conquers his heart, his imagination, who compels his faith by making other women abhorrent to him, who allures and maddens with the certainty of her power to make good his ideal of her. He cannot marry her; that animal on the bed is capable of living for twenty years.

'So much for him. A girl of twenty-eight, whose wealth and brain and beauty, and that other something that has not yet been analysed and labelled, have made her a social star; who has come to wonder, then to resent, then to yawn at the general vanity of life, is suddenly swept out of her calm orbit by a man's passion; and, with the swiftness of decision natural to her, goes to Europe. She returns in less than three months. For these two people there is but one sequel. The second chapter will be written the first time they are alone. Then they will go to Europe. What will be the rest of the book?

'First, there will be an ugly and reverberating scandal. In the course of a year or two she will compel him to return in the interest of his career. She will not be able to remain; so proud a woman could not stand the position. Again he will go with her. In a word, my friend's career will be ruined. So many novelists and reporters have written the remaining chapters of this sort of story that it is hardly worth while for me to go any further.

'So much for them. Let us consider the other victims – the children. A morphine-mother in an asylum, a father in a strange land with a woman who is not his wife, the world cognizant of all the facts of the case. They grow up at odds with society. Result, they are morbid, warped, unnormal. In trite old English, their lives are ruined, as are all lives that have not had a fair chance.'

He returned abruptly to the bedside. He laid his finger on the woman's pulse.

'No morphine tonight and she dies. A worthless wretch is sent where she belongs. Four people are saved.'

His breast swelled. His grey eyes seemed literally to send forth smoke; they suggested some noiseless deadly weapon of war. He exclaimed aloud: 'My God! what a power to lie in the hands of one man! I stand here the arbiter of five destinies. It is for *me* to say whether four people shall be happy or wretched, saved or ruined. I might say, with Nero, "I am God!" ' He laughed. 'I am famed for my power to save where others have failed. I am famed in the comic weeklies for having ruined the business of more undertakers than any physician of my day. That has been my role, my professional pride. I have never felt so proud as now.'

The woman, who had been moving restlessly for some time, twitched suddenly and uncontrollably. She opened her eyes.

'Give it to me – quick!' she demanded. Her voice, always querulous, was raucous; her eyes were wild.

'No,' he said, deliberately, 'you will have no more morphine; not a drop.'

She stared at him incredulously, then laughed.

'Stop joking,' she said, roughly. 'Give it to me – quick – quick! I am very weak.'

'No,' he said.

Then, as he continued to hold her eyes, her own gradually expanded with terror. She raised herself on one arm.

'You mean that?' she asked.

'Yes.'

He watched her critically. She would be interesting.

'You are going to cure me with drastic measures, since others have failed?'

'Possibly.'

Her face contracted with hatred. She had been a rather clever woman, and she believed that he was going to experiment with her. But she had also been a strong-willed woman and used to command since babyhood.

'Give me that morphine,' she said, imperiously. 'If you don't I'll be dead before morning.'

He stood imperturbable. She sprang from the bed and flung herself upon him, strong with anger and apprehension.

'Give it to me!' she screamed. 'Give it to me!' And she strove to bite him.

He caught her by the shoulder and held her at arm's-length. She writhed and struggled and cursed. Her oaths might have been learned in the gutter. She kicked at him and strove to reach him with her nails, clawing the air. She looked like a witch on a broomstick.

'What an exquisite bride she was!' he thought. 'And what columns of rubbish have been printed about her and her entertainments!'

The woman was shrieking and struggling.

'Give it to me! You brute! You fiend! I always hated you! Give it to me! I am dying! I am dying! Help! Help!' But the walls were padded, and she knew it.

He permitted her to fling herself upon him, easily brushing aside her jumping fingers and snapping teeth. He knew that her agony was frightful. Her body was a network of hungry nerves. The diseased pulp of her brain had ejected every thought but one. She squirmed like an old autumn leaf about to fall. Her ugly face became tragic. The words shot from her dry contracted throat: 'Give me the morphine! Give me the morphine!'

Suddenly realising the immutability of the man in whose power she was, she sprang from him and ran frantically about the room, uttering harsh bleatlike cries. She pulled open the drawers of a chest, rummaging among its harmless contents, gasping, quivering, bounding, as her tortured nerves commanded. When she had littered the floor with the contents of the chest she ran about screaming hopelessly. The doctor shuddered, but he thought of the four innocent people in her power and in his.

She fell in a heap on the floor, biting the carpet, striking out her arms aimlessly, tearing her nightgown into strips; then lay quivering, a hideous, speckled, uncanny thing, who should have been embalmed and placed beside the Venus of Milo.

She raised herself on her hands and crawled along the carpet, casually at first, as a man stricken in the desert may, half-consciously, continue his search for water. Then the doctor, intently watching her, saw an expression of hope leap into her bulging eyes. She scrambled past him towards the wash-stand. Before he could define her purpose, she had leaped upon a goblet inadvertently left there and had broken it on the marble. He reached her just in time to save her throat.

Then she looked up at him pitifully. 'Give it to me!'

She pressed his knees to her breast. The red burned-out tear-ducts yawned. The tortured body stiffened and relaxed.

'Poor wretch!' he thought. 'But what is the physical agony of a night to the mental anguish of a lifetime?'

'Once! Once!' she gasped; 'or kill me.' Then, as he stood implacable, 'Kill me! Kill me!'

He picked her up, put a fresh nightgown on her, and laid her on the bed. She remained as he placed her, too weak to move, her eyes staring at the ceiling above the big four-posted bed.

He returned to his chair and looked at his watch. 'She may live two hours,' he thought. 'Possibly three. It is only twelve. There is plenty of time.'

The room grew as still as the mountain-top whence he had that day returned. He attempted to read, but could not. The sense of supreme power filled his brain. He was the gigantic factor in the fates of four.

Then Circumstance, the outwardly wayward, the ruthlessly sequential, played him an ugly trick. His eyes, glancing idly about the room, were arrested by a big old-fashioned rocking-chair. There was something familiar about it. Soon he remembered that it resembled one in which his mother used to sit. She had been an invalid, and the most sinless and unworldly woman he had ever known. He recalled, with a touch of the old impatience, how she had irritated his active, aspiring, essentially modern mind with her cast-iron precepts of right and wrong. Her conscience flagellated her, and she had striven to develop her son's to the goodly proportion of her own. As he was naturally a truthful and upright boy, he resented her homilies mightily. 'Conscience,' he once broke out impatiently, 'has made more women bores, more men failures, than any ten vices in the rogues' calendar.'

She had looked in pale horror, and taken refuge in an axiom: 'Conscience makes cowards of us all.'

He moved his head with involuntary pride. The greatest achievement of civilisation was the triumph of the intellect over inherited impressions. Every normal man was conscientious by instinct, however he might outrage the sturdy little judge clinging tenaciously to his bench in the victim's brain. It was only when the brain grew big with knowledge and the will clasped it with fingers of steel that the little judge was throttled, then cast out.

Conscience. What was it like? The doctor had forgotten. He had never committed a murder nor a dishonourable act. Had the impulse of either been in him, his cleverness would have put it aside with a smile of scorn. He had never scrupled to thrust from his path whoever or whatever stood in his way, and had stridden on without a backward glance. His profession had involved many experiments that would have made quick havoc of even the ordinary man's conscience.

Conscience. An awkward guest for an unsuspected murderer; for the groundling whose heredity had not been conquered by brain. Fancy being pursued by the spectre of the victim!

The woman on the bed gave a start and groan that recalled him to the case in hand. He rose and walked quickly to her side. Her eyes were closed, her face was black with congested blood. He laid his finger on her pulse. It was feeble.

'It will not be long now,' he thought.

He went toward his chair. He felt a sudden distaste for it, a desire for motion. He walked up and down the room rather more rapidly than before.

'If I were an ordinary man,' he thought, 'I suppose that tortured creature on the bed would haunt me to my death. Rot! A murderer I should be called if the facts were known, I suppose. Well, she is worse. Did I permit her to live she would make the living hell of four people.'

The woman gave a sudden awful cry, the cry of a lost soul shot into the night of eternity. The stillness had been so absolute, the cry broke that stillness so abruptly and so horridly, that the doctor, strong-brained, strong-nerved as he was, gave a violent start, and the sweat started from his body.

'I am a fool,' he exclaimed angrily, welcoming the sound of his voice; 'but I wish to God it were day and there were noises outside.'

He strode hurriedly up and down the room, casting furtive glances at the bed. The night was quiet again, but still that cry rang through it and lashed his brain. He recalled the theory that sound never dies. The waves of space had yielded this to him.

'Good God!' he thought. 'Am I going to pieces? If I let this wretch, this criminal die, I save four people. If I let her live, I ruin their lives. The life of a man of brain and pride and heart; the life of a woman of beauty and intellect and honour; the lives of two children of unknown potentialities, for whom the world has now a warm heart. "The greatest good of the greatest number" – the principle that governs civil law. Has not even the worthy individual been sacrificed to it again and again? Does it not hang the criminal dangerous to the community? And is that called murder? What am I at this moment but law epitomised? Shall I hesitate? My God, am I hesitating? Conscience – is it that? A superfluous instinct transmitted by my ancestors and coddled by a woman – is it that which has sprung from its grave, rattling its bones? "*Conscience makes*" – oh, shame that I should succumb when so much is at stake – that I should hesitate when the welfare of four human beings trembles in the balance! "*Conscience*" – that in the moment of my supreme power I should falter!'

He returned to the woman. He reached his finger toward her pulse, then hurriedly withdrew it and resumed his restless march.

'This is only a nightmare, born of the night and the horrible stillness. Tomorrow in the world of men it will be forgotten, and I shall rejoice . . . But there will be recurring hours of stillness, of solitude. Will this night repeat itself? Will that thing on the bed haunt me? Will that cry shriek in my ears? Oh, shame on my selfishness! What am I thinking of? To let that base, degraded wretch exist, that I may live peaceably with my conscience? To let four others go to their ruin, that I may escape a few hours of torment? That I – *I* – should come to this! "The greatest good of the greatest number. The greatest" . . . "Conscience makes cowards of us all!" '

To his unutterable self-contempt and terror, he found his will for once powerless to control the work of the generations that had preceded him. His iron jaw worked spasmodically, his grey eyes looked frozen. The marble pallor of his face was suffused with a tinge of green.

'I despise myself!' he exclaimed, with fierce emphasis. 'I loathe myself! I will not yield! "*Conscience*" – they shall be saved, and by me. "*The greatest*" – I will maintain my intellectual supremacy – that, if nothing else. She shall die!'

He halted abruptly. Perhaps she was already dead. Then he could reach the door in a bound and run downstairs and out of the house. To be followed . . .

He ran to the bed. The woman still breathed faintly, her mouth was twisted into a sardonic and pertinent expression. His hand sought his pocket and brought forth a case. He opened it and stared at the hypodermic syringe. His trembling fingers closed about it and moved toward the woman. Then, with an effort so violent he fancied he could hear his tense muscles creak, he straightened himself and turned his back upon the bed. At the same moment he dropped the instrument to the floor and set his heel upon it.

A MONARCH
OF A SMALL SURVEY

A Monarch of a Small Survey

I

The willows haunted the lake more gloomily, trailed their old branches more dejectedly, than when Dr Hiram Webster had, forty years before, bought the ranchos surrounding them from the Moreno grandees. Gone were the Morenos from all but the archives of California, but the willows and Dr Hiram Webster were full of years and honours. The ranchos were ranchos no longer. A somnolent city covered their fertile acres, catching but a whiff at angels' intervals of the metropolis of nerves and pulse and feverish corpuscles across the bay.

Lawns sloped to the lake. At the head of the lawns were large imposing mansions, the homes of the aristocracy of the city, all owned by Dr Webster, and leased at high rental to a favoured few. To dwell on Webster Lake was to hold proud and exclusive position in the community, well worth the attendant ills. To purchase of those charmed acres was as little possible as to induce the Government to part with a dwelling-site in Yosemite Valley.

Webster Hall was twenty years older than the tributary mansions. The trees about it were large and densely planted. When storms tossed the lake they whipped the roof viciously or held the wind in longer wails. There was an air of mystery about the great rambling sombre house; and yet no murder had been done there, no traveller had disappeared behind the sighing trees to be seen no more, no tale of horror claimed it as birthplace. The atmosphere was created by the footprints of time on a dwelling old in a new land. The lawns were unkempt, the bare windows stared at the trees like unlidded eyes. Children ran past it in the night. The unwelcomed of the spreading city maintained that if nothing ever had happened there something would; that the place spoke its manifest destiny to the least creative mind.

The rain poured down one Sunday morning, splashing heavily on the tin of the oft-mended roof, hurling itself noisily through the trees. The doctor sat in his revolving-chair before the desk in his study. His yellow face was puckered; even the wrinkles seemed to wrinkle as he whirled about every few moments and scowled through the trees at the flood racing down the lawn to the lake. His thin mouth was a trifle relaxed, his clothes hung loose upon him; but the eyes, black and sharp as a ferret's, glittered undimmed.

He lifted a large bell that stood on the desk and rang it loudly. A maidservant appeared.

'Go and look at the barometer,' he roared. 'See if this damned rain shows any sign of letting up.'

The servant retired, reappeared, and announced that the barometer was uncompromising.

'Well, see that the table is set for twenty, nevertheless; do you hear? If they don't come I'll raise their rents. Send Miss Webster here.'

His sister entered in a few moments. She was nearly his age, but her faded face showed wrinkles only on the brow and about the eyes. It wore a look of haunting youth; the expression of a woman who has grown old unwillingly, and still hopes, against reason, that youth is not a matter of a few years at the wrong end of life. Her hair was fashionably arranged, but she was attired in a worn black silk, her only ornament a hair brooch. Her hands were small and well-kept, although the skin hung loose upon them, spotted with the moth-patches of age. Her figure was erect, but stout.

'What is it, brother?' she asked softly, addressing the back of the autocrat's head.

He wheeled about sharply.

'Why do you always come in like a cat? Do you think those people will come today? It's raining cats and dogs.'

'Certainly; they always come, and they have their carriages – '

'That's just it. They're getting so damned high-toned that they'll soon feel independent of me. But I'll turn them out, bag and baggage.'

'They treat you exactly as they have treated you for thirty years and more, brother.'

'Do you think so? Do you think they'll come today?'

'I am sure they will, Hiram.'

He looked her up and down, then said, with a startling note of tenderness in his ill-used voice: 'You ought to have a new frock, Marian. That is looking old.'

Had not Dr Webster been wholly deficient in humour he would

have smiled at his sister's expression of terrified surprise. She ran forward and laid her hand on his shoulder.

'Hiram,' she said, 'are you – you do not look well today.'

'Oh, I am well enough,' he replied, shaking her off. 'But I have noticed of late that you and Abigail are looking shabby, and I don't choose that all these fine folks shall criticise you.' He opened his desk and counted out four double-eagles.

'Will this be enough? I don't know anything about women's things.'

Miss Webster was thankful to get any money without days of expostulation, and assured him that it was sufficient. She left the room at once and sought her companion, Miss Williams.

The companion was sitting on the edge of the bed in her small ascetic chamber, staring, like Dr Webster downstairs, through the trees at the rain. So she had sat the night of her arrival at Webster Hall, then a girl of eighteen and dreams. So she had sat many times, feeling youth slip by her, lifting her bitter protest against the monotony and starvation of her existence, yet too timid and ignorant to start forth in search of life. It was her birthday, this gloomy Sunday. She was forty-two. She was revolving a problem – a problem she had revolved many times before. For what had she stayed? Had there been an unadmitted hope that these old people must soon die and leave her with an independence with which she could travel and live? She loved Miss Webster, and she had gladly responded to her invitation to leave the New England village, where she was dependent on the charity of relatives, and make her home in the new country. Miss Webster needed a companion and housekeeper; there would be no salary, but a comfortable home and clothes that she could feel she had earned. She had come full of youth and spirit and hope. Youth and hope and spirit had dribbled away, but she had stayed, and stayed. Today she wished she had married any clod in her native village that had been good enough to address her. Never for one moment had she known the joys of freedom, of love, of individuality.

Miss Webster entered abruptly.

'Abby,' she exclaimed, 'Hiram is ill.' And she related the tale of his unbending.

Miss Williams listened indifferently. She was very tired of Hiram. She accepted with a perfunctory expression of gratitude the gold piece allotted to her. 'You are forty-two, you are old, you are nobody,' was knelling through her brain.

'What is the matter?' asked Miss Webster, sympathetically; 'have you been crying? Don't you feel well? You'd better dress, dear; they'll be here soon.'

She sat down suddenly on the bed and flung her arms about her companion, the tears starting to her kindly eyes.

'We are old women,' she said. 'Life has not meant much to us. You are younger in years, but you have lived in this dismal old house so long that you have given it and us your youth. You have hardly as much of it now as we have. Poor girl!'

The two women fondled each other, Abby appreciating that, although Miss Webster might not be a woman of depths, she too had her regrets, her yearnings for what had never been.

'What a strange order of things it is,' continued the older woman, 'that we should have only one chance for youth in this life! It comes to so many of us when circumstances will not permit us to enjoy it. I drudged – drudged – drudged, when I was young. Now that I have leisure and – and opportunity to meet people, at least, every chance of happiness has gone from me. But you are comparatively young yet, really; hope on. The grave will have me in a few years, but you can live and be well for thirty yet. Ah! if I had those thirty years!'

'I would give them to you gladly for one year of happiness – of youth.'

Miss Webster rose and dried her eyes. 'Well,' she said, philosophically, 'regrets won't bring things. We've people to entertain today, so we must get out of the dumps. Put on your best frock, like a good child, and come down.'

She left the room. Miss Williams rose hurriedly, unhooked a brown silk frock from the cupboard, and put it on. Her hair was always smooth; the white line of disunion curved from brow to the braids pinned primly above the nape of the neck. As she looked into the glass today she experienced a sudden desire to fringe her hair, to put red on her cheeks; longing to see if any semblance of her youthful prettiness could be coaxed back. She lifted a pair of scissors, but threw them hastily down. She had not the courage to face the smiles and questions that would greet the daring innovation, the scathing ridicule of old man Webster.

She stared at her reflection in the little mirror, trying to imagine her forehead covered with a soft fringe. Nothing could conceal the lines about the eyes and mouth, but the aging brow could be hidden from critical gaze, the face redeemed from its unyouthful length. Her cheeks were thin and colourless, but the skin was fine and smooth. The eyes, which had once been a rich dark blue, were many shades lighter now, but the dullness of age had not possessed them yet. Her set mouth had lost its curves and red, but the teeth were good. The head was finely shaped and well placed on the low old-fashioned shoulders. There were no contours now under the stiff frock. Had her estate been high she would have been, at the age of forty-two, a youthful and pretty woman. As it was, she was merely an old maid with a patrician profile.

She went downstairs to occupy her chair in the parlour, her seat at the table, to be overlooked by the fine people who took no interest whatever in the 'Websters' companion'. She hated them all. She had watched them too grow old with a profound satisfaction for which she reproached herself. Even wealth had not done for them what she felt it could have done for her.

The first carriage drove up as she reached the foot of the stair. The front door had been opened by the maid as it approached, and the rain beat in. There was no *porte-cochère*; the guests were obliged to run up the steps to avoid a drenching. The fashionable Mrs Holt draggled her skirts, and under her breath anathematised her host.

'It will be the happiest day of my life when this sort of thing is over,' she muttered. 'Thank heaven, he can't live much longer!'

'Hush!' whispered her prudent husband; Miss Webster had appeared.

The two women kissed each other affectionately. Everybody liked Miss Webster. Mrs Holt, an imposing person, with the rigid backbone of the newly rich, held her hostess's hand in both her own as she assured her that the storm had not visited California which could keep her from one of dear Dr Webster's delightful dinners. As she went upstairs to lay aside her wrappings she relieved her feelings by a facial pucker directed at a painting, on a matting panel, of the doctor in the robes of Japan.

The other guests arrived, and after making the pilgrimage upstairs, seated themselves in the front parlour to slide up and down the horsehair furniture and await the entrance of the doctor. The room was funereal. The storm-ridden trees lashed the bare dripping windows. The carpet was threadbare. White crocheted tidies lent their emphasis to the hideous black furniture. A table with marble top, like a graveyard slab, stood in the middle of the room. On it was a bunch of wax flowers in a glass case. On the white plastered walls hung family photographs in narrow gilt frames. In a conspicuous place was the doctor's diploma. In another, Miss Webster's first sampler. 'The first piano ever brought to California' stood in a corner, looking like the ghost of an ancient spinet. Miss Williams half expected to find it some day standing on three legs, resting the other.

Miss Webster sat on a high-backed chair by the table, nervously striving to entertain her fashionable guests. The women huddled together to keep warm, regardless of their expensive raiment. The men stood in a corner, reviling the mid-day dinner in prospect. Miss Williams drifted into a chair and gazed dully on the accustomed scene. She had looked on it weekly, with barely an intermission, for a quarter of a century. With a sensation of relief, so sharp that it seemed to underscore the hateful monotony of it all, she observed that there was a young person in the company. As a rule, neither threats nor bribes could bring the young to Webster Hall. Then she felt glad that the young person was a man. She was in no mood to look on the blooming hopeful face of a girl.

He was a fine young fellow, with the supple lean figure of the college athlete, and a frank attractive face. He stood with his hands plunged into his pockets, gazing on the scene with an expression of ludicrous dismay. In a moment he caught the companion's eye. She smiled involuntarily, all that was still young in her leaping to meet that glad symbol of youth. He walked quickly over to her.

'I say,' he exclaimed, apologetically, 'I haven't been introduced, but do let ceremony go, and talk to me. I never saw so many old fogies in my life, and this room is like a morgue. I almost feel afraid to look behind me.'

She gave him a grateful heartbeat for all that his words implied.

'Sit down,' she said, with a vivacity she had not known was left in her sluggish currents. 'How – did – you – come – here?'

'Why, you see, I'm visiting the Holts – Jack Holt was my chum at college – and when they asked me if I wanted to see the oldest house in the city, and meet the most famous man "on this side of the bay", why, of course, I said I'd come. But, gods! I didn't know it would be like this, although Jack said the tail of a wild mustang couldn't get him through the front door. Being on my first visit to the widely renowned California, I thought it my duty to see all the sights. Where did you come from?'

'Oh, I live here. I've lived here for twenty-four years.'

'Great Scott!' His eyes bulged. 'You've lived in this house for twenty-four years?'

'Twenty-four years.'

'And you're not dead yet – I beg pardon,' hastily. 'I am afraid you think me very rude.'

'No, I do not. I am glad you realise how dreadful it is. Nobody else ever does. These people have known me for most of that time, and it has never occurred to them to wonder how I stood it. Do you know that you are the first young person I have spoken with for years and years?'

'You don't mean it?' His boyish soul was filled with pity. 'Well, I should think you'd bolt and run.'

'What use? I've stayed too long. I'm an old woman now, and may as well stay till the end.'

The youth was beginning to feel embarrassed, but was spared the effort of making a suitable reply by the entrance of Dr Webster. The old man was clad in shining broadcloth, whose maker was probably dead these many years. He leaned on a cane heavily mounted with gold.

'Howdy, howdy, howdy?' he cried, in his rough but hospitable tones. 'Glad to see you. Didn't think you'd come. Yes, I did, though,' with a chuckle. 'Well, come down to dinner, I'm hungry.'

He turned his back without individual greeting, and led the way along the hall, then down a narrow creaking stairway to the basement dining-room, an apartment as stark and cheerless as the parlour, albeit the silver on the table was very old and heavy, the linen unsurpassed.

The guests seated themselves as they listed, the youngster almost clinging to Miss Williams. The doctor hurriedly ladled the soup, announcing that he had a notion to let them help themselves, he was so hungry. When he had given them this brief attention he supplied his own needs with the ladle direct from the tureen.

'Old beast!' muttered Mrs Holt. 'It's disgusting to be so rich that you can do as you please.'

But for this remark, delivered as the ladle fell with a clatter on the empty soup-plate, the first course was disposed of amidst profound silence. No-one dared to talk except as the master led, and the master was taking the edge off his appetite.

The soup was removed and a lavish dinner laid on the table. Dr Webster sacrificed his rigid economic tenets at the kitchen door, but there was no rejoicing in the hearts of the guests. They groaned in spirit as they contemplated the amount they should be forced to consume at one of the clock.

The doctor carved the turkeys into generous portions, ate his, then began to talk.

'Cleveland will be re-elected,' he announced dictatorially. 'Do you hear? Harrison has no show at all. What say?' His shaggy brows rushed together. He had detected a faint murmur of dissent. 'Did you say he wouldn't, John Holt?'

'No, no,' disclaimed Mr Holt, who was a scarlet Republican. 'Cleveland will be re-elected beyond a doubt.'

'Well, if I hear of any of you voting for Harrison! I suppose you think I can't find out what ticket you vote! But I'll find out, sirs. Mark my words, Holt, if you vote the Republican ticket – '

He stopped ominously and brought his teeth together with a vicious click. Holt raised his wine-glass nervously. The doctor held his note to a considerable amount.

'The Republican party is dead – dead as a doornail,' broke in an unctuous voice. A stout man with a shrewd time-serving face leaned forward. 'Don't let it give you a thought, doctor. What do you think of the prospects for wheat?'

'Never better, never better. They say the Northern crops will fail, but it's a lie. They can't fail. You needn't worry, Meeker. Don't pull that long face, sir; I don't like it.'

'The reports are not very encouraging,' began a man of bile and nerves and melancholy mien. 'And this early rain – '

'Don't contradict me, sir,' cried Webster. 'I say they can't fail. They haven't failed for eight years. Why should they fail now?'

'No reason at all, sir – no reason at all,' replied the victim, hurriedly. 'It does me good to hear your prognostications.'

'I hear there is a slight rise in Con. Virginia,' interposed Mrs Holt, who had cultivated tact.

'Nonsense!' almost shouted the tyrant. The heavy silver fork of the Morenos fell to his plate with a crash. 'The mine's as rotten as an old lung. There isn't a handful of decent ore left in her. No more clodhoppers'll get rich out of that mine. You haven't been investing, have you?' His ferret eyes darted from one face to another. 'If you have, don't you ever darken my doors again! I don't approve of stock-gambling, and you know it.'

The guests, one and all, assured him that not one of their hard-earned dollars had gone to the stockmarket.

'Great Scott!' murmured the youth to Miss Williams; 'is this the way he always goes on? Have these people no self-respect?'

'They're used to him. This sort of thing has gone on ever since I came here. You see, he has made this lake the most aristocratic part of the city, so that it gives one great social importance to live here; and as he won't sell the houses, they have to let him trample on their necks, and he loves to do that better than he loves his money. But that is not the only reason. They hope he will leave them those houses when he dies. They certainly deserve that he should. For years, before they owned carriages, they would tramp through wind and rain every Sunday in winter to play billiards with him, to say nothing of the hot days of summer. They have eaten this mid-day dinner that they hate time out of mind. They have listened to his interminable yarns, oft repeated, about early California. In all these years they have never contradicted him, not once. They thought he'd die long ago, and now they're under his heel, and they couldn't get up and assert themselves if they tried. All they can do is to abuse him behind his back.'

'It all seems disgusting to me.'

His independent spirit was very attractive to the companion.

'I'd like to bluff him at his own game, the old slave-driver,' he continued.

'Oh don't! don't!' she quavered.

She was, in truth, anxiously awaiting the moment when Dr Webster should see fit to give his attention to the stranger.

He laughed outright.

'Why, what makes you so afraid of him? He doesn't beat you, does he?'

'It isn't that. It's the personality of the man, added to force of habit.'

'Well, Mr Strowbridge,' cried Dr Webster, suddenly addressing the youth, 'what are you doing for this world? I hear you are just out of Harvard University. University men never amount to a row of pins.'

Strowbridge flushed and bit his lip, but controlled himself.

'Never amount to a row of pins,' roared the doctor, irritated by the haughty lifting of the young man's head. 'Don't even get any more book-learning now, I understand. Nothing but football and boat-racing. Think that would make a fortune in a new country? Got any money of your own?'

'My father, since you ask me, is a rich man – as well as a gentle-man,' said Strowbridge, with the expression of half-frightened anger of the righteously indignant, who knows that he has not the advantages of cool wit and scathing repartee, and, in consequence, may lose his head. 'He inherited his money, and was not forced to go to a new country and become a savage,' he blurted out.

Mr Holt extended himself beneath the table, and trod with terrified significance on Strowbridge's foot. Miss Williams fluttered with terror and admiration. The other guests gazed at the youth in dismay. For the first time in the history of Webster Hall the grizzly had been bearded in his lair.

'Sir! sir!' spluttered Webster. Then he broke into a roar. 'Who asked this cub here, anyway? Who said you could write and ask permission to bring your friends to my house? How dare you – how dare you – how dare you, sir, speak to me like that? Do you know, sir – '

'Oh, I know all about you,' exclaimed Strowbridge, whose young blood was now uncontrollable. 'You are an ill-bred, purse-proud old tyrant, who wouldn't be allowed to sit at a table in California if it wasn't for your vulgar money.' He pushed back his chair and stood up. 'I wish you good-day, sir. I pity you. You haven't a friend on earth. I also apologise for my rudeness. My only excuse is that I couldn't help it.'

And he went hurriedly from the room.

To Miss Williams the feeble light went with him. The appalled guests attacked their food with feverish energy. Dr Webster stared stupidly at the door; then his food gave out the sound of ore in a crusher. He did not speak for some time. When he did he ignored the subject of young Strowbridge. His manner was appreciably milder – somewhat dazed – although he by no means gave evidence of being humbled to the dust. The long dinner dragged to its close. The women went up to the parlour to sip tea with Miss Webster and slide up and down the furniture. The men followed the doctor to the billiard-room. They were stupid and sleepy, but for three hours they were forced alternately to play and listen to the old man's anecdotes of the days when he fought and felled the grizzly. He seemed particularly anxious to impress his hearers with his ancient invincibility.

That night, in the big four-posted mahogany bed in which he had been born, surrounded by the massive ugly furniture of his old New England home, Dr Webster quietly passed away.

2

Not only the lakeside people, but all of the city with claims to social importance attended the funeral. Never had there been such an imposing array of long faces and dark attire. Miss Webster being prostrated, the companion did the honours. The dwellers on the lake occupied the post of honour at the head of the room, just beyond the expensive casket. Their faces were studies. After Miss Williams had exchanged a word with each, Strowbridge stepped forward and bent to her ear.

'Oh, I say,' he whispered, eagerly, 'I have to tell some member of this family how sorry I am for losing my temper and my manners the other day. It was awfully fresh of me. Poor old boy! Do say that you forgive me.'

A smile crept between her red lips.

'He had a good heart,' she said. 'He would have forgiven you.' And then the long and impressive ceremony began.

All the great company followed the dead autocrat to the cemetery, regardless of the damaging skies. Miss Williams, as chief mourner, rode in a hack, alone, directly behind the hearse. During the dreary ride she laboured conscientiously to stifle an unseemly hope. In the other carriages conversation flowed freely, and no attempt was made to discourage expectations.

Two evenings later, as the crowd of weary businessmen boarded the train that met the boat from the great city across the bay, it was greeted as usual by the cry of the local newsboys. This afternoon the youngsters had a rare bait, and they offered it at the top of their shrill worn voices: 'Will of Dr Hiram Webster! Full account of Dr Hiram Webster's lastwillundtestermint.'

A moment later the long rows of seats looked as if buried beneath an electrified avalanche of newspapers. At the end of five minutes the papers were fluttering on the floor amid the peanut-shells and orange-skins of the earlier travellers. There was an impressive silence, then an animated, terse, and shockingly expressive conversation. Only a dozen or more sat with drawn faces and white lips. They were the dwellers by the lake. Hiram Webster had left every cent of his large fortune to his sister.

For two weeks Webster Lake did not call on the heiress. It was too sore. At the end of that period philosophy and decency came to the rescue. Moreover, cupidity: Miss Webster too must make a will, and before long.

They called. Miss Webster received them amiably. Her eyes were red, but the visitors observed that her mourning was very rich; they had never seen richer. They also remarked that she held her grey old head with a loftiness that she must have acquired in the past two weeks; no one of them had ever seen it before. She did not exactly patronise them; but that she appreciated her four millions there could be no doubt.

Strowbridge glanced about in search of Miss Williams. She was not in the room. He sauntered out to the garden and saw her coming from the dairy. She wore a black alpaca frock and a dark apron. Her face was weary and sad.

'Could anyone look more hopeless!' he thought. 'The selfish old curmudgeon, not to leave her independent! How her face can light up! She looks almost young.'

For she had seen him and hastened down the path. As he asked after her health and said that he had been looking for her, she smiled and flushed a little. They sat down on the steps and chatted until approaching voices warned them that both pleasure and duty were over. She found herself admitting that she had been bitterly disappointed to learn that she was still a dependant, still chained to the gloomy mansion by the lake. Yes; she should like to travel, to go to places she had read of in the doctor's library – to live. She flushed with shame later when she reflected on her confidences – she who was so proudly reticent. And to a stranger! But she had never met anyone so sympathetic.

Many were the comments of the visitors as they drove away.

'Upon my word!' exclaimed Mrs Holt; 'I do believe Marian Webster will become stuck-up in her old age.'

'Four millions are a good excuse,' said Mrs Meeker, with a sigh.

'That dress did not cost a cent under three hundred dollars,' remarked a third, with energy. 'And it was tried on four times, if it was once. She is evidently open to consolation.'

But Miss Webster had by no means ceased to furnish material for comment. A month later Mrs Meeker burst in on Mrs Holt. 'What do you think?' she cried. 'Old Miss Webster is refurnishing the house from top to bottom. I ran in just now, and found everything topsy-turvy. Thompson's men are there frescoing – frescoing! All the carpets have been taken up and are not in sight. Miss Webster informed me that she would show us what she could do, if she was seventy-odd, but that she didn't want anyone to call until everything was finished. Think of that house being modernised – that old whited sepulchre!'

Mrs Holt had dropped the carriage-blanket she was embroidering for her daughter's baby. 'Are you dreaming?' she gasped. 'Hiram will haunt the place!'

'Just you wait. Miss Webster hasn't waited all these years for nothing.'

Nor had she. The sudden and stupendous change in her fortunes had routed grief – made her dizzy with possibilities. She had no desire to travel, but she had had a lifelong craving for luxury. She might not have many more years to live, she reiterated to Miss Williams, but during those years her wealth should buy her all that her soul had ever yearned for.

In due course the old exclusive families of the infant city received large squares of pasteboard heavily bordered with black, intimating that Miss Webster would be at home to her friends on Thursdays at four of the clock. On the first Thursday thereafter the parlour of Webster Hall was as crowded as on the day of the funeral. 'But who would ever know the old barrack?' as the visitors whispered. Costly lace hid the window-panes, heavy pale-blue satin the ancient frames. The walls were frescoed with pink angels rising from the tinting clouds of dawn. The carpet was of light-blue velvet; the deep luxurious chairs and divans and the *portières* were of blue satin. The wood-work was enamelled with silver. Out in the wide hall Persian rugs lay on the inlaid floors, tapestry cloth hid the walls. Carved furniture stood in the niches and the alcoves. Through the open doors of the library the guests saw walls upholstered with leather, low bookcases, busts of marble and bronze. An old laboratory off the doctor's study had been transformed into a dining-room, as expensive and conventional as the other rooms. There a dainty luncheon was spread.

Miss Webster led the lakeside people upstairs. The many spare bedrooms had been handsomely furnished, each in a different colour. When the guests were finally permitted to enter Miss Webster's own virgin bower their chins dropped helplessly. Only this saved them from laughing outright.

The room was furnished as for a pampered beauty. The walls were covered with pink silk shimmering under delicate lace. The white enamel bed and dressing-table were bountifully draped with the same materials. Light filtered through rustling pink. The white carpet was sprinkled with pink roses. The trappings of the dressing-table were of crystal and gold. In one corner stood a Psyche mirror. Two tall lamps were hooded with pink.

All saw the humour; none the pathos.

The doctor's room had been left untouched. Sentiment and the value of the old mahogany had saved it. Miss Williams's room was also the same little cell. She assisted to receive the guests in a new black silk gown. Miss Webster was clad from head to foot in English crêpe, with deep collar and girdle of dull jet.

That was a memorable day in the history of the city.

Thereafter Miss Webster gave an elaborate dinner-party every Sunday evening at seven o'clock. No patient groans greeted her invitations. Never did a lone woman receive such unflagging attentions.

At each dinner she wore a different gown. It was at the third that she dazzled her guests with an immense pair of diamond earrings. At the fourth they whispered that she had been having her nails manicured. At the fifth it was painfully evident that she was laced. At the sixth they stared and held their breath: Miss Webster was unmistakably painted. But it was at the tenth dinner that they were speechless and stupid: Miss Webster wore a blond wig.

'They can just talk all they like,' said the lady to her companion that last night, as she sat before her mirror regarding her aged charms. 'I have four millions, and I shall do as I please. It's the first time I ever could, and I intend to enjoy every privilege that wealth and independence can give. Whose business is it, anyway?' she demanded, querulously.

'No-one's. But it is a trifle ridiculous, and you must expect people to talk.'

'They'd better talk!' There was a sudden suggestion of her brother's personality, never before apparent. 'But why is it ridiculous, I should like to know? Hasn't a woman the right to be young if she can? I loved Hiram. I was a faithful and devoted sister; but he took my youth, and now that he has given it back, as it were, I'll make the most of it.'

'You can't be young again.'

'Perhaps not, in years; but I'll have all that belongs to youth.'

'Not all. No man will love you.'

Miss Webster brought her false teeth together with a snap. 'Why not, I should like to know? What difference do a few years make? Seventy is not much, in any other calculation. Fancy if you had only seventy dollars between you and starvation! Think of how many thousands of years old the world is! I have now all that makes a woman attractive – wealth, beautiful surroundings, scientific care. The steam is taking out my wrinkles; I can see it.'

She turned suddenly from the glass and flashed a look of resentment on her companion.

'But I wish I had your thirty years' advantage. I do! I do! Then they'd see.'

The two women regarded each other in silence for a long moment. Love had gone from the eyes and the hearts of both. Hate, unacknowledged as yet, was growing. Miss Webster bitterly envied the wide gulf between old age and her quarter-century companion and friend. Abigail bitterly envied the older woman's power to invoke the resemblance and appurtenances of youth, to indulge her lifelong yearnings.

When the companion went to her pillow that night she wept passionately. 'I will go,' she said. 'I'll be a servant; but I'll stay here no longer.'

The next morning she stood on the veranda and watched Miss Webster drive away to market. The carriage and horses were unsurpassed in California. The coachman and footman were in livery. The heiress was attired in lustreless black silk elaborately trimmed with jet. A large hat covered with plumes was kept in place above her painted face and red wig by a heavily dotted veil – that crier of departed charms. She held a black lace parasol in one carefully gloved hand. Her pretty foot was encased in patent leather.

'The old fool!' murmured Abby. 'Why, oh, why could it not have been mine? I could make myself young without being ridiculous.'

She let her duties go and sauntered down to the lake. Many painted boats were anchored close to ornamental boat-houses. They seemed strangely out of place beneath the sad old willows. The lawns were green with the green of spring. Roses ran riot everywhere. The windows of the handsome old-fashioned houses were open, and Abby was afforded glimpses of fluttering white gowns, heard the tinkle of the mandolin, the cold precise strains of the piano, the sudden uplifting of a youthful soprano.

'After all, it only makes a little difference to them that they got nothing,' thought the companion, with a sigh.

A young man stepped from one of the long windows of the Holt mansion and came down the lawn. Miss Williams recognised Strowbridge. She had not seen him for several weeks; but he had had his part in her bitter moments, and her heart beat at sight of him today.

'I too am a fool,' she thought. 'Even with her money my case would be hopeless. I am nearly double his age.'

He jumped into a boat and rowed down the lake. As he passed the Webster grounds he looked up and saw Abby standing there.

'Hulloa!' he called, as if he were addressing a girl of sixteen. 'How are you, all these years? Jump in and take a row.'

He made his landing, sprang to the shore and led her to the boat with the air of one who was not in the habit of being refused. Abby had no inclination to suppress him. She stepped lightly into the boat, and a moment later was gliding down the lake, looking with admiring eyes on the strong young figure in its sweater and white trousers. A yachting-cap was pulled over his blue eyes. His face was bronzed. Abby wondered if many young men were as handsome as he. As a matter of fact, he was merely a fine specimen of young American manhood, whose charm lay in his frank manner and kindness of heart.

'Like this?' he asked, smiling into her eyes.

'Yes, indeed. Hiram used to row us sometimes; but the boat lurched so when he lost his temper that I was in constant fear of being tipped over.'

'Hiram must have been a terror to cats.'

'A what?'

'Beg pardon! Of course you don't know much slang. Beastly habit.'

He rowed up and down the lake many times, floating idly in the long recesses where the willows met overhead. He talked constantly; told her yarns of his college life; described boat-races and football matches in which he had taken part. At first his only impulse was to amuse the lonely old maid; but she proved such a delighted and sympathetic listener that he forgot to pity her. An hour passed, and with it her bitterness. She no longer felt that she must leave Webster Hall. But she remembered her duties, and regretfully asked him to land her.

'Well, if I must,' he said. 'But I'm sorry, and we'll do it again some day. I'm awfully obliged to you for coming.'

'Obliged to me? – You?' she said, as he helped her to shore. 'Oh, you don't know –' And laughing lightly, she went rapidly up the path to the house.

Miss Webster was standing on the veranda. Her brows were together in an ugly scowl.

'Well!' she exclaimed. 'So you go gallivanting about with boys in your old age! Aren't you ashamed to make such an exhibition of yourself?'

Abby felt as if a hot palm had struck her face. Then a new spirit, born of caressed vanity, asserted itself.

'Wouldn't you have done the same if you had been asked?' she demanded.

Miss Webster turned her back and went up to her room. She locked the door and burst into tears. 'I can't help it,' she sobbed, helplessly. 'It's dreadful of me to hate Abby after all these years; but – those terrible thirty! I'd give three of my millions to be where she is. I used to think she was old, too. But she isn't. She's young! Young! – A baby compared to me. I could more than be her mother. Oh, I must try as a Christian woman to tear this feeling from my heart.'

She wrote off a check and directed it to her pastor, then rang for the trained nurse her physician had imported from New York, and ordered her to steam and massage her face and rub her old body with spirits of wine and unguents.

Strowbridge acquired the habit of dropping in on Miss Williams at all hours. Sometimes he called at the dairy and sat on a corner of the table while she superintended the butter-making. He liked her old-fashioned music, and often persuaded her to play for him on the new grand piano in the sky-blue parlour. He brought her many books by the latter-day authors, all of them stories by men about men. He had a young contempt for the literature of sentiment and sex. Even Miss Webster grew to like him, partly because he ignored the possibility of her doing otherwise, partly because his vital frank personality was irresistible. She even invited him informally to dinner; and after a time he joked and guyed her as if she were a schoolgirl, which pleased her mightily. Of Miss Williams he was sincerely fond.

'You are so jolly companionable, don't you know,' he would say to her. 'Most girls are bores; don't know enough to have anything to talk about, and want to be flattered and flirted with all the time. But I feel as if you were just another fellow, don't you know.'

'Oh, I am used to the role of companion,' she would reply.

With the first days of June he returned to Boston, and the sun turned grey for one woman.

Life went its way in the old house. People became accustomed to the spectacle of Miss Webster rejuvenated, and forgot to flatter. It may be added that men forgot to propose, in spite of the four millions. Deeper grew the gulf between the two women. Once in every week Abby vowed she would leave, but habit was too strong. Once in every week Miss Webster vowed she would turn the companion out, but dependence on the younger woman had grown into the fibres of her old being.

Strowbridge returned the following summer. Almost immediately he called on Miss Williams.

'I feel as if you were one of the oldest friends I have in the world, don't you know,' he said, as they sat together on the veranda. 'And I've brought you a little present – if you don't mind. I thought maybe you wouldn't.'

He took a small case from his pocket, touched a spring, and revealed a tiny gold watch and fob. 'You know,' he had said to himself apologetically as he bought it, 'I can give it to her because she's so much older than myself. It's not vulgar, like giving handsome presents to girls. And then we are friends. I'm sure she won't mind, poor old thing!' Nevertheless, he looked at her with some apprehension.

His misgivings proved to be vagaries of his imagination. Abby gazed at the beautiful toy with radiant face. 'For me!' she exclaimed – 'that lovely thing? And you really bought it for me?'

'Why, of course I did,' he said, too relieved to note the significance of her pleasure. 'And you'll take it?'

'Indeed I'll take it.' She laid it on her palm and looked at it with rapture. She fastened the fob in a buttonhole of her blouse, but removed it with a shake of the head. 'I'll just keep it to look at, and only wear it with my black silk. It's out of place on this rusty alpaca.'

'What a close-fisted old girl the Circus must – '

'Oh, hush, hush! She might hear you.' Abby rose hastily. 'Let us walk in the garden.'

They sauntered between the now well-kept lawns and flowerbeds and entered a long avenue of fig trees. The purple fruit hung abundantly among the large green leaves. Miss Williams opened one of the figs and showed Strowbridge the red luscious pith.

'You don't have these over there.'

'We don't. Are they good to eat this way?'

She held one of the oval halves to his mouth.

'Eat!' she said.

And he did. Then he ate a dozen more that she broke for him.

'I feel like a greedy schoolboy,' he said. 'But they are good, and no mistake. You have introduced me to another pleasure. Now let us go and take a pull.'

All that afternoon there was no mirror to tell her that she was not the girl who had come to Webster Hall a quarter of a century before. That night she knelt long by her bed, pressing her hands about her face.

'I am a fool, I know,' she thought, 'but such things have been. If only I had a little of her money.'

The next day she went down to the lake, not admitting that she expected him to take her out; it would be enough to see him. She saw him. He rowed past with Elinor Holt, the most beautiful girl of the lakeside. His gaze was fixed on the flushed face, the limpid eyes. He did not look up.

Miss Williams walked back to the house with the odd feeling that she had been smitten with paralysis and some unseen force was propelling her. But she was immediately absorbed in the mani-fold duties of the housekeeping. When leisure came reaction had preceded it.

'I am a fool,' she thought. 'Of course he must show Elinor Holt attention. He is her father's guest. But he might have looked up.'

That night she could not sleep. Suddenly she was lifted from her thoughts by strange sounds that came to her from the hall without. She opened the door cautiously. A white figure was flitting up and down, wringing its hands, the grey hair bobbing about the jerking head.

'No use!' it moaned. 'No use, no use, no use! I'm old, old, old! Seventy-four, seventy-four, seventy-four! Oh, Lord! Oh, Lord! Oh, Lord! Thy ways are past finding out. Amen!'

Abby closed her door hurriedly. She felt the tragedy out there was not for mortal eyes to look upon. In a few moments she heard the steps pause before her door. Hands beat lightly upon it.

'Give me back those thirty years!' whimpered the old voice. 'They are mine! You have stolen them from me!'

Abby's hair rose. 'Is Marian going mad?' she thought.

But the next morning Miss Webster looked as usual when she appeared, after her late breakfast in bed, bedecked for her drive to market. She had modified her mourning, and wore a lavender cheviot, and the parasol and hat were in harmony with all but herself.

'Poor old caricature!' thought Abby. 'She makes me feel young.'

A week later, when the maid entered Miss Webster's bedroom at the accustomed morning hour, she found that the bed had not been occupied. Nor was her mistress visible. The woman informed Miss Williams at once, and together they searched the house. They found her in her brother's room, in the old mahogany bed in which she too had been born. She was dead. Her grey hair was smooth under her lace nightcap. Her hands were folded, the nails glistening in the dusky room. Death had come peacefully, as to her brother. What had taken her there to meet it was the last mystery of her strange old soul.

3

Again a funeral in the old house, again a crowd of mourners. This time there was less ostentation of grief, for no-one was left worth impressing. The lakeside people gathered, as before, at the upper end of the parlour and gossiped freely. 'Miss Williams ought to have put the blond wig on her,' said Mrs Holt. 'I am sure that is what Marian would have done for herself. Poor Marian! She was a good soul, after all, and really gave liberally to charity. I wonder if she has left Miss Williams anything?'

'Of course. She will come in for a good slice. Who is better entitled to a legacy?'

Pertinent question! They exchanged amused glances. Words were superfluous, but Mrs Holt continued: 'I think we are pretty sure of our shanties this time; Marian was really fond of us, and had neither kith nor kin; but I, for one, am going to make sure of some memento of the famous Webster estate.' And she deliberately opened a cabinet, lifted down a small antique teapot, and slipped it into her bag.

The others laughed noiselessly. 'That is like your humour,' said Mrs Meeker. Then all bent their heads reverently. The ceremony had begun.

Two days later Miss Williams wandered restlessly up and down the hall waiting for the evening newspaper. She made no attempt to deceive herself this time. She thought tenderly of the dead, but she was frankly eager to learn just what position in the world her old friend's legacy would give her. Two or three times she had been on the point of going to a hotel; but deeply as she hated the place, the grip of the years was too strong. She felt that she could not go until the law compelled her.

'I cannot get the capital for ten months,' she thought, 'but I can get the income, or borrow; and I can live in the city, or perhaps – But I must not think of that.'

A boy appeared at the end of the walk. His arms were full of newspapers, and he rolled one with expert haste. Miss Williams could contain, herself no further. She ran down the walk. The boy gave the paper a sudden twist and threw it to her. She caught it and ran upstairs to her room and locked the door. For a moment she turned faint. Then she shook the paper violently apart. She had not far to search. The will of so important a personage as Miss Webster was necessarily on the first page. The 'story' occupied a column, and the contents were set forth in the headlines. The headlines read as follows:

WILL OF MISS MARIAN WEBSTER – SHE LEAVES HER
VAST FORTUNE TO CHARITY – FOUR MILLIONS THE
PRICE OF ETERNAL FAME – NO LEGACIES

The room whirled round the forgotten woman. She turned sick, then cold to her marrow. She fell limply to the floor, and crouched there with the newspaper in her hand. After a time she spread it out on the floor and spelled through the dancing characters in the long column. Her name was not mentioned. Those thirty years had out-weighed the devotion of more than half a lifetime. It was the old woman's only revenge, and she had taken it.

No tears came to Miss Williams's relief. She gasped occasionally. 'How could she? How could she? How could she?' her mind reiter-ated. 'What difference would it have made to her after she was dead? And I – oh God – what will become of me?' For a time she did not think of Strowbridge. When she did, it was to see him smiling into the eyes of Elinor Holt. Her delusion fell from her in that hour of terrible realities. Had she read of his engagement in the newspaper before her she would have felt no surprise. She knew now what had brought him back to California. Many trifles that she had not noted at the time linked themselves symmetrically together, and the chain bound the two young people.

'Fool! fool!' she exclaimed. 'But no – thank heaven, I had that one little dream! – the only one in forty-three years!'

The maid tapped at her door and announced dinner. She bade her go away. She remained on the floor, in the dark, for many hours. The stars were bright, but the wind lashed the lake, whipped the trees against the roof. When the night was half done she staggered to her feet. Her limbs were cramped and numbed. She opened the door and listened. The lights were out, the house was still. She limped over to the room which had been Miss Webster's. That too was dark. She lighted the lamps and flooded the room with soft pink light. She let down her hair, and with the old lady's long scissors cut a thick fringe. The hair fell softly, but the parting of years was obtrusive. A bottle of gum tragacanth stood on one corner of the dressing-table, and with its contents Abby matted the unneighbourly locks together. The fringe covered her careworn brow, but her face was pallid, faded. She knew where Miss Webster had kept her cosmetics. A moment later an array of bottles, jars, and rouge-pots stood on the table before her.

She applied the white paint, then the red. She darkened her eye-lashes, drew the lip-salve across her pale mouth. She arranged her soft abundant hair in a loose knot. Then she flung off her black frock, selected a magnificent white satin dinner-gown from the wardrobe, and put it on. The square neck was filled with lace, and it hid her skinny throat. She put her feet into French slippers and drew long gloves up to her elbows. Then she regarded herself in the Psyche mirror.

Her eyes glittered. The cosmetics, in the soft pink light, were the tintings of nature and youth. She was almost beautiful.

'That is what I might have been without aid of art had wealth been mine from the moment that care of nature's gifts was necessary,' she said, addressing her image. 'I would not have needed paint for years yet, and when I did I should have known how to use it! I need not have been old and worn at forty-three. Even now – even now – if wealth were mine, and happiness!' She leaned forward, and pressing her finger against the glass, spoke deliberately; there was no passion in her tones: 'When that letter came twenty-five years ago offering me a home, I wish I had flouted it, although I did not have five dollars in the world. I wish I had become a harlot – a harlot! do you hear? Nothing – nothing in life can be as bad as life empty, wasted, emotionless, stagnant! I have existed forty-three years in this great, beautiful, multiform world, and I might as well have died at birth for all that it has meant to me. Nature gave me abundantly of her instincts. I could have been a devoted wife, a happy mother, a gay and careless harlot! I would have chosen the first, but failing that – rather the last a thousand times than this! For then I should have had some years of pleasure, excitement, knowledge – '

She turned abruptly and started for the door, stopped, hesitated, then walked slowly to the wardrobe. She unhooked a frock of nun's veiling and tore out the back breadths. She returned to the mirror and fastened the soft flowing stuff to her head with several of the dead woman's ornamental pins.

For a few moments longer she gazed at herself, this time silently. Her eyes had the blank look of introspection. Then she went from the house and down to the lake.

The next day the city on the ranchos was able to assure itself comfortably that Webster Lake had had its tragedy.

Of the Tragedy it knew nothing.

THE TRAGEDY OF A SNOB

The Tragedy of a Snob

The first twenty-three years of Andrew Webb's life were passed in that tranquillity of mind and body induced by regular work, love of exercise, and a good digestion. He lived in a little flat in Harlem, with his widowed mother and a younger sister who was ambitious to become an instructor of the young and to prove that woman may be financially independent of man. At that time Andrew's salary of thirty dollars a week, earned in a large savings-bank of which he was one of many book-keepers, covered the family's needs. Mr Webb had died when his son was sixteen, leaving something under two thousand dollars and a furnished flat in Harlem. For a time the outlook was gloomy. Andrew left school and went to work. Good at figures, stoically steady, he rose by degrees to command a fair remuneration. A brother of Mrs Webb, currently known as 'Uncle Sandy Armstrong', lived in miserly fashion on the old homestead in New Jersey. Occasionally he sent his sister a ten-dollar bill. Mrs Webb, believing him to be as straitened as herself, albeit without a family, never applied to him for assistance. Twice a year she dutifully visited him and put his house in order. Her children rarely could be induced to accompany her. They detested their fat garrulous unkempt uncle, and only treated him civilly out of the goodness of their hearts and respect for their mother. On Christmas Day he invariably dined with them, and his meagre presents by no means atoned for his atrocious table-manners.

The family in the flat was a happy one, despite the old carpets, the faded rep furniture, the general air of rigid economy, and the inevitable visits of Uncle Sandy. Mrs Webb was sweet of temper, firm of character, sound of health. Her cheeks and eyes were faded, her black dress was always rusty, her general air that of a middle-class gentlewoman who bore her reverses bravely. Polly was a plump bright-eyed girl, with a fresh complexion and her mother's evenness of temper. In spite of her small allowance, she managed to dress in the prevailing style. She had barely emerged from short frocks when she took a course of lessons in dressmaking, she knew how to bargain, and spent the summer months replenishing her own and her mother's wardrobe. Mrs Webb did the work of the flat, assisted by an Irish maiden who came in by the day: there was no place in the flat for her to sleep.

Andrew was the idol of the family. He supported them, and he was a thoroughly good fellow; he had no bad habits, and they had never seen him angry. His neighbours were regularly made acquainted with the proud fact that he walked home from his office in lower Broadway every afternoon in the year, 'except Sundays and during his vacation', as his mother would add. She was a conscientious woman. Moreover, they thought him very handsome. He was five feet ten, lean, and athletic in appearance. It is true that his head was narrow and his face cast in a heavy mould; but there was no superfluous flesh in his cheeks, and his thick skin was clean. Like his sister, he managed to dress well. He was obliged to buy his clothes ready-made, but he had the gift of selection.

When the subtle change came, his mother and sister uneasily confided to each other the fear that he was in love. As the years passed, however, and he brought them no new demand upon their affections and resources, they ceased to worry, and finally to wonder. Andrew was not the old Andrew; but, if he did not choose to confide the reason, his reserve must be respected. And at least it had affected neither his generosity nor his good temper. He still spent his evenings at home, listened to his mother or Polly read aloud, and never missed the little supper of beer and crackers and cheese before retiring.

2

One morning, while Webb was still one with his little family, he read, as was usual with him on the long ride down-town, his Harlem edition of one of the New York dailies. He finished the news, the editorials, the special articles: nothing was there to upset the equilibrium of his life. His attention was attracted, as he was about to close the paper, by a long leaded 'story' of a ball given the night before by some people named Webb. Their superior social importance was made manifest by the space and type allotted them, by the fact that their function was not held over for the Sunday issue, and by the imposing rhetoric of the headlines.

Andrew read the story with a feeling of personal interest. From that moment, unsuspected by himself, the readjustment of his mind to other interests began – the divorce of his inner life from the simple conditions of his youth.

Thereafter he searched the Society columns for accounts of the doings of the Webb folk. Thence, by a natural deflection, he became generally interested in the recreations of the great world: he acquired a habit, much to his sister's delight, of buying the weekly chronicles of Society, and all the Sunday issues of the important dailies.

At first the sparkle and splendour, the glamour and mystery of the world of fashion dazzled and delighted him. It was to him what fairy-tales of prince and princess are to children. For even he, prosaic, phlegmatic, with nerves of iron and brain of shallows, had in him that germ of the picturesque which in some natures shoots to high and full-flowered ideals, in others to lofty or restless ambitions, coupled with a true love of art; and yet again develops a weed of tenacious root and coarse enduring fibre which a clever maker of words has named snobbery.

Gradually within Andrew's slow mind grew a dull resentment against Fate for having played him so sinister a trick as to give him the husk without the kernel, a title without a story that anyone would ever care to read. Why, when one of those Webb babies was due – the family appeared to be a large one – could not his little wandering ego have found its way into that ugly but notable mansion on Fifth Avenue instead of having been spitefully guided to a New Jersey farm? Not that Andrew expressed himself in this wise. Had he put his thoughts into words, he would probably have queried in good terse English: 'Why in thunder can't I be Schuyler Churchill Webb instead of a nobody in Harlem? He's just my age, and I might as well have been he as not.'

His twenty-third birthday cake, prepared by loving hands, had scarcely been eaten when the waves of snobbery first lapped his feet. At twenty-five they had broken high above his head, and the surge was ever in his ears. He was not acutely miserable: his health was too perfect, his appetite too good. But deeper and deeper each week did he bury his perplexed head in the social folklore of New York and Newport. Oftener and oftener during the city season did he promenade central Fifth Avenue from half-past four until half-past five in the afternoon of pleasant days. He lived for the hour which would find him sauntering from Forty-first Street to the Park and back again. He knew all the fashionable men and women by sight. There was no-one to tell him their names, but the names themselves were more familiar than the rows of figures in his books down-town. He fitted them to such presences as seemed to demand them as their right. He grew into a certain intimacy with the slender trimly accoutred girls who held themselves so erectly and wore their hair with such maidenly severity. They were so different in appearance from all the women he had known or seen, and from the languishing creatures in his mother's cherished *Book of Beauty*, that he came to look upon them as a race apart, which they were; as something not quite human, which was a slander. As they stalked along so briskly in their tailor-made frocks, their cheeks and eyes brilliant with health, the average observer would have likened them to healthy high-bred young racehorses.

On the whole, however, Andrew gave the full measure of his admiration to the women who took their exercise less violently. When the spring came, and the Park was green, he would stand in the plaza, surrounded by its great hotels, the deep rumble of the avenue behind him, forgetting even the phalanxes of tramping girls, with their accessories of boys and poodles. Before him were the wide gates of the Park, the green wooded knolls rolling away – almost to his home in Harlem. Just beyond the gates was a bend in the driveway, and he never tired of watching the stream of carriages wind as from a cavern and roll out to the avenue. The vivid background claimed as its own those superb traps with their dainty burdens of women who held their heads so haughtily, whose plumage was so brilliant. The horses glittered and pranced. The parasols fluttered like butterflies above the flower-faces beneath. Webb would stand entranced, bitterly thankful that there was such a scene for him to look upon, choking back a sob that he had no part in it.

When summer came and Society flitted to Newport, that paradise in which he only half believed, he was more lonely and glum than the loneliest and glummest and most *blasé* clubman, who clung to his window because he hated Newport and could not afford London. Quite accidentally, when his infatuation was about three years old, he came into a singular compensation. In the summer, during his ten days' vacation, when he was tramping through the woods, he fell in with a party of Western people, who manifested much interest in New York. To Andrew there was only one New York, and with that his soul was identified. Insensibly, he began to talk of New York Society as if it were part of his daily experience. His careful, if restricted, study of its habits had made him sufficiently familiar with it to enable him to deceive the wholly ignorant. He described the people, their brilliant 'functions', the individualities of certain of its members. He talked freely of Ward McAllister, and imitated that gentleman's peculiarities of thought and speech, so familiar to the newspaper reader. For the time he deceived himself as well as his hearers; and so fascinating did he find this delusion, that he remained with the inquisitive and guileless party until the end of his vacation. After that he made it a point each year to attach himself to some party of tourists, and to tell them of New York Society, plus Andrew Webb. He was not a liar in the ordinary sense of the word. In his home and in the bank where he played his daily game of give-and-take, his reputation for veracity was enviable. Every mortal not an idiot has his day-dreams. Webb merely dreamed his aloud to an audience. And these summers were the oases of his life.

He had one other pleasure equally keen. On the first day of each month he dined at Del Monico's. In the beginning it meant the forfeit of his usual stand-up luncheon, but he had decided that the cause was worthy of the sacrifice. One evening, however, he lingered on upper Fifth Avenue longer than usual, and entered late. The restaurant was crowded. He stood at the door, hesitating, knowing that he would not be permitted to seat himself at a table already occupied by even one person. Suddenly a small common-looking little man came forward and touched his arm.

'Won't you share my table?' he said, effusively. 'My name's Slocum, and I've seen you here often. You mustn't go away. Come in.'

Andrew gratefully accepted, and followed Mr Slocum over to the little table on the other side of the room.

'I say,' said Slocum, after Webb had ordered his dinner, 'I've hit on a plan. It's been in my head for some time. How often do you come here?'

'Once a month.'

'That's my game exactly. I'm a clerk on a small salary; but I must have one good dinner a month, if I don't have my hair cut. Now, suppose we dine together. One portion's enough for two, and the same dinner'll only cost each of us half what it does now. See?'

Andrew did not take kindly to Mr Slocum: the vulgar young man was so different from the magnificent creatures about him. But the offer was not to be ignored, and he closed with it. For the following three years, until he was twenty-eight, he dined regularly at Del Monico's, and in that rarefied atmosphere his head gently swam. He forgot the flat in Harlem – forgot that he was Andrew, not Schuyler Churchill Webb.

3

One day word came that 'Uncle Sandy Armstrong' was dead. Andrew could not get away, nor Polly, who was then a teacher; but Mrs Webb hastily packed an old carpet-bag and went over to superintend her brother's funeral. That evening the young people discussed the death of their relative in a businesslike manner, which their mother would have resented, but which was justifiable from their point of view.

'I suppose ma will have the farm,' remarked Polly, still a plump, rosy, and well-dressed Polly, albeit with an added air of importance and a slightly didactic enunciation. 'How much do you suppose it's worth?'

Andrew, who was lying on the sofa smoking a pipe, protruded his upper lip. 'Four thousand – not a cent more. The orchard's all gone to seed, and the house too.'

'We might mortgage the land, and fit the house up for summer boarders.'

Andrew frowned heavily. His sister was absently tapping a pile of compositions on the table beside her, and did not see the frown. She would not have suspected the cause if she had.

'As well that as anything,' he replied, indifferently. 'No-one will buy it, that's positive, with all that marsh.'

Two days later he returned home to find the very atmosphere of the place quivering with excitement. Bridget stood in the doorway of the kitchen, which faced the end of the narrow hallway personal to the Webb abode. Her round eyes glittered in a purple face. She waved her arms wildly.

'Oh, Mr Webb!' she began.

'Andrew, come here,' shrieked Polly from the other end of the hall. 'Come here, quick!'

It was not Webb's habit to move rapidly; but, fearing that his mother was ill, he walked briskly to the parlour. Mrs Webb, trembling as from a recent nervous shock, her face flushed, a legal document in her lap, sat in an upright chair, apparently in the best of health. Polly was on the verge of hysterics.

'What do you think has happened?' she cried. 'Tell him, ma; I can't.' Then she flung herself face downward on the sofa and kicked her heels together.

'We are rich, Andrew,' said Mrs Webb, with a desperate effort at calmness. 'Your Uncle Sandy has been investing and doubling money these twenty years. He has left one hundred and fifty thousand dollars – fifty thousand to each of us.'

Andrew's knees gave way. He sat down suddenly. He had but one thought. A radiant future flashed the little room out of vision. That would be his which for five years he had desired with all the insidious force of a fixed idea.

'Say something, Andrew, for heaven's sake!' cried Polly, 'or I shall scream. Fifty thousand dollars all my own! No more school, no more dress-making! We'll all go to Europe. Ma says it's well invested, and we shall have four thousand a year each. Goodness – goodness – goodness me!'

'I should like to fit up the old house and live there,' said Mrs Webb. 'But – yes – I should like to see Europe first. That was one of the dreams of my youth.'

'And I'll have a sealskin! At last! You shall have a magnificent black silk and a pair of diamond earrings – '

'Polly!' exclaimed her mother, 'what should I do with diamonds? A new black silk – a rich one – yes, I shall like that. Poor Sandy!'

Andrew leaned forward and took the document and laid it on his knee. He stroked it as tenderly as if it had been a woman's head and he another man. There was no sentiment in his nature, although he was an admirer of beauty – New York beauty. After a time he detached himself from his thoughts and talked the matter over with his mother and sister. When they asked him what he should do he replied, confusedly, that he did not know. But the plans of neither were so well defined as his.

All that night he sat on the edge of his bed staring at the worn outlines of the boy and the dog on the rug under his feet. Fifty thousand dollars! It seemed a great fortune to him. Such a sum had been familiar enough in figures for many years. But that it might represent a concrete wad of bills was a fact which had never pre-sented itself to his imagination before. Fifty thousand dollars! He did not know what the objects of his idolatry were worth, merely that they were idle and luxurious. These fifty thousand dollars would enable him to be idle and luxurious – and to meet society at last on its own ground.

4

The interval between that night and the day upon which the estate was settled, Andrew passed in a sort of impatient dream. Never before had days, weeks, months seemed so long; never had he so dissociated himself from his little world and melted into that luminous circle of which he was to become a component part. How he was to obtain his passport into fashionable society was a question that did not concern him. Its portals were typified to him by the wide gates of Central Park, through which all might roll upon whom fortune smiled. One blessed fact possessed his mind: by the first of July he should be master of his future, liberated from his desk, free to go to Newport. When his foot actually pressed that reservation, all the rest would come about quite naturally. At this time he still preserved his self-respect. He felt quite the equal of the men he had brushed elbows with at Del Monico's – the pink-faced youths with their butter-coloured tops, the affable elderly men with their bulbous stomachs and puffy eyes. And he had caught many of their little fads. He had risen in the night, and opening the door connecting the kitchen and dining-room, that he might have sufficient scope, he had practised the remarkable gait of the New York youth of fashion: that slight forward inclination of the shoulders, that slighter crab-like angle of the body, that ponderous thoughtful tread: the only difference from the walk of the 'tough' being in the length of the step. One hand was in a pocket, the other absently manipulated a stick. He had also witnessed the handshake, and of his proficiency in this accomplishment he felt assured.

On the third day of July, one hour after the law had yielded up its temporary foundling, he ordered an elaborate outfit from the most fashionable tailor in New York. This order and others drilled a large hole in his first quarter's income, but he regarded that as a trifling detail. His mother and sister were meanwhile selling the homely necessities of their flat at auction, as the first step to a year abroad. They wondered at Andrew's desire to go to Newport, but had heard that it was a pretty place with a good bathing-beach, and much visited by tourists. They spent the last night together in a hotel; and Mrs Webb, in spite of a faint protest from Andrew, ordered beer and crackers and cheese. They had eaten this little supper for many years, and the women, who were very tearful, insisted that this last evening together must be as much like the dear old evenings as possible. It was a sad meal.

5

It was a profoundly hot August day when Andrew left the steamboat and actually stood upon Newport soil. More properly, he stood upon a plank wharf, and was not impressed with the dock. But as the omnibus rolled through the town his heart began to swell, his rather dull eyes to glow. The hour was two, and the city asleep under its ivy and flowers. After New York, it seemed deliciously quiet, and old, and aristocratic. The pounding of the horses' hoofs, the voices of the people in the omnibus, were desecrating. He had glimpses of long avenues, dark, green, dim; a flash of villa top or imposing gateway behind the stately trees. He felt that he was in paradise.

He was in a mood to admire the hotel, plain and unpretending structure as it was; it was so old and still and highly respectable. He descended from the omnibus nervously and went into the office. A clerk handed him a pen, and he registered his name in a clerkly hand, 'A. Armstrong Webb'. He had decided to acknowledge his debt to his uncle and add a cubit to his stature at the same time. The clerk wheeled the book round, glanced indifferently at the name, and handed a key to a bell-boy. Webb, conscious of a faint chill, followed the boy upstairs. The room to which he was conducted was an ordinary one overlooking the area. He had been treated as any commonplace and unknown traveller would be. The thought increased the chill; then he philosophically concluded that a noble-man travelling incognito would be treated in the same way, and went downstairs to the dining-room. There he was somewhat surprised to find that dinner was being served instead of luncheon. He had supposed that dinner in a Newport hotel would be served at eight o'clock.

After dinner he went out to the veranda, sat himself on one of the chairs by the railing, and smoked an expensive cigar. He was beginning to feel strangely lonely. There seemed to be very few people in the hotel, and he experienced his first pang of helplessness, of doubt. He had supposed that the hotel would be full of great people. As he glanced down the avenue, those big houses seemed like tombs – buried, themselves, under a rank growth of foliage. And it was so wondrous quiet!

His cigar cheered him somewhat, and he sauntered back to the office and entered into conversation with the clerk, a good-humoured little Englishman with cheeks like his own apples. The clerk knew at a glance that the stranger was neither a 'swell' nor a frequenter of

Newport; but he liked his manly appearance, and readily met his advances. To his dismay, Webb learned that the 'swells' no longer went to the hotels; or, if obliged to do so for a short period, secluded themselves in their rooms. They lived in cottages. Oh yes! all those fine houses were called cottages. It was a sort of fad – American modesty, the clerk supposed. There was not much fun of any sort at the hotel until the fifteenth, when a good many tourists came. Oh yes! there were some people there, mostly old ones, who had come every season for many years, he believed. Rather depressing parties, these; they looked so old-fashioned, and didn't do much to brighten up things.

Webb, with growing dejection, left the hotel and strolled up the avenue. There his spirits revived. The avenue was so beautiful, so gloomy, so old! He drew in deep inhalations of its unmistakably aristocratic atmosphere. He felt its subtle possessing influence. Once more his imagination awakened. He leaned on a Gothic gateway and gazed upon a superb Queen Anne cottage with Tudor towers. Incongruities in architecture mattered nothing to him. He precipitated his astral part through the massive door and wandered, with ponderous, thoughtful tread, over the deep carpets of the drawing-rooms and corridors. He drank tea on the back veranda with languid dames and with men who had never stood at desks. He threw himself into an armchair and listened to a slim-waisted smooth-haired girl coquetting with the piano. He sat with the haughty chatelaine and talked of – there his imagination failed him. He hardly knew what these people talked of, although he had read many society novels. As far as his memory served him, they talked of nothing in particular. He wandered down the avenue, dreaming his dream at many gate-posts. He saw no-one, but thereby was the illusion deepened. Newport for the hour was his.

He returned to the hotel veranda, lit another cigar, and was about to meditate upon some plan of campaign, when suddenly an odd and delightful thing happened. It was four-and-thirty of the clock. As if to the ringing of a bell and the rising of a curtain, Bellevue Avenue became suddenly alive with carriages. The big gates seemed to yawn simultaneously and discharge their expensive freight. It was as if these actors in the Newport drama would lose their weekly salary did they step on the boards a moment too late. The avenue, with its gay frocks and parasols, was like a long flower-bed in spring. Webb's cigar went out. He leaned forward eagerly, straining his eyes.

In some of the superb traps were decrepit old dowagers wagging their feeble heads, wondering, perhaps, how much longer their millions would keep them alive. Sometimes their young heirs were with them, patient and placid. Others were pitifully alone. Several men were on horseback, riding in the agonised fashion of the day. There were carriages full of girls with complexions of ivory and claret, air of ineffable daintiness. Now and then a victoria would roll by in which women lolled, heavily veiled with crape. Webb wondered if they really could sorrow like common folks. Mingling with the superb turnouts were barouches unmistakably hired, occupied by people dressed with a certain cheap smartness. Here and there a girl, probably of the people, cantered half-defiantly down the line, a sailor-hat on her head, her jacket open over a shirt and 'four-in-hand'. Once a yoke of oxen, driven by a bareheaded maid, straggled into the throng.

The avenue before the hotel became deserted once more. The upper end was blocked with carriages, all apparently bent in the same direction. Andrew ran down the steps, half inclined to follow, half fearing they would never return. A number of open hacks stood before the hotel. A driver immediately approached Andrew.

'Like a drive, sir?'

'Yes,' said Webb. 'Go where the others are going.'

'Certainly, sir. And, if you be a stranger, I can tell you most of the names.'

Andrew could have tipped him on the spot. He should be able to identify those people at last! He felt that he had advanced another step!

'We'll drive slow and meet them on their return,' said the driver. He indicated with a gesture of contempt a passing carriage.

'You see them, sir? They be people that comes to the hotels and goes away and talks about spending the summer in Newport. But anyone could tell that they're just hotel people, and that the hack is hired. They don't deceive nobody here.'

The words gave Andrew a hint for which he was thankful. He understood that he must not stay at the hotel. Where should he go, however? He must take a 'cottage', he supposed.

They rolled down a thick-leaved avenue and out over the stubby sand-hills by the sea. Here and there a large mansion crowned the heights, and Andrew was glad to see the traditional cottage in full relief. He paid it scant attention, however. The procession of carriages had already turned, and his faithful guide uttered many a name which sounded like old sweet music in his ears. Some of the younger faces were unfamiliar; but they, too, bore names that the newspapers had made famous.

'Now look with all your eyes,' cried the driver, suddenly. 'Here's Mrs Johnny Belhaven. She's worth more millions than all the rest put together, and is an A1 whip.'

A plump but distinguished-looking woman bore down on them in what appeared to be a chariot. Andrew had never seen anything so high on wheels before. Mrs Belhaven looked down upon her 'Order' as from a throne, and wore a slightly supercilious expression.

'And there's Ward McAllister,' continued the driver, excitedly; 'him as is the leader of the Four Hundred, you know.'

Andrew almost raised himself from his seat. He stared with bulging eyes at the tired carelessly dressed elderly man with whom he had been intimate so many years.

He returned to the hotel. His spirits were normal again. He had taken his part in a fragment of the daily life of Newport. As he passed through the office on his way to the elevator, the clerk beckoned to him.

'As you seem a stranger, sir,' he said, apologetically, 'I thought I would introduce you to Mr Chapman. He's the correspondent of several New York papers, and could tell you how to amuse yourself.'

A short thickset amiable young man shook Andrew's hand heartily. Mr Chapman was not the sort of person Andrew had gone to Newport to meet, but he was glad of any friendship, temporarily.

The two young men went out to the veranda. Andrew proffered his new cigar-case. The other accepted gratefully. He was the freelance correspondent of several New York weekly papers, and his salary was not large. He tipped his chair back, put his feet on the railing, and confided to Webb that he hated Newport.

'I wouldn't have come here this summer if I could have got out of it,' he said, gloomily. 'It's my third year, and the place gets worse every season. These people are so stuck-up there's no approaching them for news. Even Lancaster, who has a sort of *entrée* because he is connected with a swagger family, admits that it's as much as his life is worth to get anything out of them. He's the correspondent of the New York *Eye*. What's worse, they don't do anything. Here it is the third of August, and not a ball has been given – just little things among themselves that you can't get at. It's enough to drive a fellow to drink. I've faked till my poor imagination is worn to a thread; the papers have to have news. But I've done one big thing this summer –

a corking beat. Did you notice half-way down the avenue a new
house surrounded by a big stone wall? That's the new Belhaven
house. They'd sworn that no reporter should so much as pass the
gates, no paper should ever show an eager world the interior of that
marble mausoleum. The newspapers were wild. Even Lancaster
had no show. I was bound that I'd get into that house, if I had to go
as a burglar. And I did, but not that way. I bribed their butcher to
let me dress up as his boy; took a camera, and photographed the
house and grounds from the seclusion of the meat-wagon. I flirted
with the cook and got her to show me the drawing-rooms. It was
early, and the family wasn't up. I dodged the butler and took snap-
shots. The other newspaper men were ready to brain me. I felt
sorry for some of them, but I had joy over Lancaster. He'd bribed
the caterer and florist to keep their best bits of news for him. A low
trick that; not but what I'd do it myself if I had his salary. He got a
scoop last year, and you couldn't speak to him for a month after.
Mrs Foster – she's one of the biggest guns, you know, a regular
cannon – refurnished her house last summer, and all the New
York papers wanted photographs. She went cranky, and said they
shouldn't have them. Wouldn't even listen to Lancaster's pleadings. But he hadn't jollied the butler for nothing. She didn't
stop here last summer – only came down every two weeks
and rearranged every stick of the furniture. The butler was nearly
distracted. It was as much as his place was worth to have her find
any of the chairs out of place, and the rooms had to be swept. So he
hit on a plan. He bought a camera and photographed the rooms
every time Mrs Foster came down. One day he met Lancaster on
the avenue and confided his method of keeping up with the old
lady. You may be sure Lancaster was not long getting a set of those
photos. It cost the newspaper a pot of money, for the butler was no
fool. But there they were next Sunday. And Mrs Foster doesn't
know to this day how it was done.'

Webb listened with mingled amusement and dismay. He was
slowly beginning to realise the determined segregation, from the
common herd, of these people, to whom he had come so confidently
to offer homage. He changed the subject.

'I don't want to stay here, don't you know,' he said, glancing
scornfully over his shoulder at the hotel which in its day had housed
the most distinguished in the land. 'What would you advise? Take
a cottage?'

'Take a cottage!' Mr Chapman fairly gasped. 'Are you a millionaire in disguise? If you were, I don't believe you could get one. The swells shut up theirs when they don't come, or let them to their friends. The others are mostly taken year after year by the same people. No; I'll tell you what you want – a bachelor's apartment. They are not so easy to get either, but I happen to know of one. It was rented four years ago by Jack Delancy, but he blew in most of his money, and then tried to recuperate on cordage. The bottom fell out of that, and now goodness knows where he is. At all events, his apartment is to let. Suppose we go now and see it. There's no time to lose.'

Andrew assented willingly, profoundly thankful that he had met Mr Chapman. The apartment was near the hotel. They found it still vacant, furnished with a certain bold distinction. The rent was high, but Andrew stifled the economic promptings of his nature, and manfully signed a check. That night there was nothing to be seen in Newport, not even a moon. The city was like a necropolis. Andrew gratefully employed his leisure hunting for servants. The following day he was comfortably installed and had invited the fortunate Mr Chapman to dinner. He found that gentleman next morning on the beach, taking snap shots at the bathers.

'This sort of thing goes,' Chapman said, 'although these people are just plain tourists. I label them "the beautiful Miss Brown", or "the famous Miss Jones", and the average reader swallows it, to say nothing of the fact that it makes the paper look well. The swells won't go in with the common herd, and want the ocean fenced in too, as it were. There are some of them over there in their carriages, taking a languid interest in the scene because they've nothing better to do. But they'd no more think of getting out and sitting on this balcony, as they do at Narragansett, than they'd ride in a streetcar. Want to go up to the Casino and see the stage go off? That's one of the sights.'

Andrew had spent a half-hour the evening before gazing at the graceful brown building which had long been a part of his dreams. He welcomed the prospect of seeing a phase of its brilliant life.

They reached the Casino a few minutes before the coach started. A large round-shouldered man, with face and frame of phlegmatic mould, occupied the seat and swung his whip with a bored and absent air. Two or three girls, clad in apotheosised organdie, and close hats, were already on top of the coach. An elderly beau was assiduously attending upon a young woman who was about to mount the ladder. She was a plain girl, with an air of refined health, and simply clad in white.

'She's worth sixteen million dollars in her own right,' said Chapman, with a groan.

On the sidewalk, between the Casino and the coach, were two groups of girls. One group gazed up at their friends on the coach, wishing them good-fortune; the other gazed upon the first, eagerly and enviously. Andrew looked from one to the other. The girls who talked to those on the coach wore organdie frocks of simple but marvellous construction. Shading their young pellucid eyes, their bare polished brows, were large Leghorn hats covered with expensive feathers or flowers. Air, carriage, complexion, manner, each was a part of the unmistakable uniform of the New York girl of fashion. But the others? Andrew put the question to Chapman.

'Oh, they're natives. We call them that to distinguish them from the cottagers. They get close whenever they get a chance, and copy the cottagers' clothes and manners. But it doesn't take a magnifying-glass to see the difference.'

Andrew looked with a pity he did not admit was fellow-feeling at the pretty girls with their bright complexions, their merely stylish clothes – which reminded him of Polly's – the inferior feathers in their chip hats. The sharp contrast between the two groups of girls was almost painful.

'I've got to leave you,' said Chapman; 'but I'll see you later. Take care of yourself.'

The horn tooted, the whip cracked, the coach started. The men on the club balcony above the Casino watched it lazily. The street between the coach and the green wall opposite had been blocked with carriages that now rolled away.

Webb turned his attention to the group of cottagers. One of the girls wore a yellow organdie trimmed with black velvet ribbons, a large Leghorn covered with yellow feathers and black velvet. She was not pretty, but she had 'an air', and that was supremest beauty in Andrew's eyes. Another was in lilac, another in pink. Each had the same sleek brown hair, the same ivory complexion. In attendance was a tall, clumsily built but very imposing young man with sleepy blue eyes and a mighty mustache. The girls paid him marked attention.

They chatted for a few moments, then walked through the entrance of the Casino, over the lawn, towards the lower balcony of the horseshoe surrounding it. Andrew followed, fascinated. The young man in attendance walked after the manner of his kind, and Andrew, unconsciously imitating him, ascended the steps, seated himself with an air of elaborate indifference opposite the party in the narrow semicircle, and composed his face into an expression of blank abstraction. His trouble was wasted: they did not see him. They had an air of seeing no-one in the world but their kind. One of the girls, to Andrew's horror, crossed her knees and swung her foot airily. The young man sank into a slouching position. Another girl joined the group, but he did not rise when introduced, nor offer to get her a chair. She was obliged to perform that office, at some difficulty, for herself.

The band began to play. Andrew leaned forward, gazing at the floor, intent upon hearing these people actually converse. But their talk only came to him in snatches between the rise and fall of the music. Like many other New-Yorkers, he had a deaf ear.

'My things disappear so – ' (from the yellow girl) . . . 'I suspect my maid wears them . . . Don't really know what I have . . . Don't dare say anything.' This was said with a languid drawl which Andrew thought delicious.

All laughed.

'Shall you go to Paris this year?'

'I don't know . . . till time comes . . . Then we keep four servants up all night packing . . . Must have some new gowns . . . You know how you have to talk to Ducet and Paquin yourself.'

The young man went to sleep. The girls put their heads together and whispered. After a time they arose with a little capricious air, which completed Andrew's subjugation, and strolled away.

6

That evening, as he sat with Chapman over the coffee in the stately little dining-room of the victim of cordage, the journalist remarked suddenly: 'I say, old fellow, you don't seem to be in it. Don't you know anybody here at all?'

Andrew shook his head gloomily.

'Well, you'll have a stupid time, I'm afraid. There are only three classes of people that come to Newport – the swells, the people who want to see the swells, and the correspondents whose unhappy fate it is to report the doings of the swells. Now, what on earth did you come here for?'

Andrew had not a confiding nature, but he could not repress a dark flush. The astute little journalist understood it.

'It's too bad you didn't bring a letter or two. One would have made it easy work. You look as well as any of them, and you've got the boodle. Where did you come from, anyway?'

'New York.'

Chapman puckered his lips about his cigar. 'That's bad. It's harder for a non-commissioned New-Yorker to get into society than for a district-attorney to get into heaven. Didn't you make any swagger friends at college?'

'I never went to college.'

'Too bad! A man should always strain a point to get to college. If he's clever he can make friends there that he can "work" for the rest of his life.'

Little by little, with adroit use of the detective faculty of the modern reporter, he extracted from Webb the tale of his years – even the extent of his fortune. The young aspirant's ingenuousness made him gasp more than once; but he had too kindly a nature to state to Webb the hopelessness of his case. His new friend was manly and generous, and had won from him a sincere liking, tempered with pity. Better let him find out for himself how things stood; then, when his eyes were open, steer him out of his difficulties.

He rose in a few moments. 'Well,' he said, cheerily, 'I wish I were Lancaster. I might be able to do something for you: but I'm not in it – not for a cent. You may as well take in the passing show, however. The first Casino hop is on tonight. Put on your togs and go.'

'Anybody there?' asked Andrew, loftily.

'Oh, rather. All the cottagers will be there, or a goodly number of them. And it's a pretty sight.'

'But how can I get in?'

'By paying the sum of one dollar, old man.'

Andrew's cigar dropped from his mouth.

'Do you mean to say that *they* go to a place and dance – in full dress – on the floor – with everybody? Why, anyone can pay a dollar.'

Chapman laughed. 'Oh! – well – go and see how it is for yourself. Meet me in the gallery at ten, and I'll tell you who's who. *Au revoir*.'

* * *

At half-past nine Andrew stood before his mirror and regarded himself meditatively. Without vanity, he could admit that so far as appearance counted he would be an ornament to any ballroom. His strong young figure carried its evening clothes with the air of a gentleman, not of a waiter. He had seen fashionable men in Del Monico's who needed their facial tresses to avoid confusion. Chapman had that day pointed out to him two scions of distinguished name whose 'sideboards' had caused him to mistake them for coachmen. He stroked his own mustache. It had never been cut, and was as silken as the hair of the ladies he worshipped. His head had been cropped by the most fashionable barber in New York. He wore no jewels. In a word, he was correct, and he assured himself of the fact with proud humility. Nevertheless, his heart was heavy behind his irreproachable waistcoat.

From his apartment it was but a few steps to the Casino. He walked there without injury to his pumps, bought his ticket at the office, half fearing that it would be refused him, and sauntered across the lawn to the inner door of the ballroom. The horseshoe was brilliantly lighted, and, with its airy architecture, looked as if awaiting a revel of the fairies. The cottagers, Andrew understood, would alight at an outside door. They were subscribers, and the office was not for them.

He went up to the gallery to await his friend. It was less than a fourth occupied by pretty girls – 'natives', he recognised at once. Some wore hats, others were in local substitute for full dress – a muslin or Indian silk turned away at the throat, a flower in the hair. He took a chair before the railing. The one beside him was occupied by a handsome dark-eyed girl who had made a brave attempt to be smart. She wore a red silk frock and a red rose in her rough abundant hair. Round her white throat she had gracefully arranged some silk lace. Andrew paid that tribute to her charms of one whose eyes have been too long accustomed to great works of art to take any interest in the chromo. Nevertheless, he was young and she was young. They flirted mildly until Chapman came in and introduced them.

'Miss Leslie is an old friend of mine, Webb,' he said in his hearty way. 'I hope you will be friends too.'

Miss Leslie bowed and beamed and flashed her pretty teeth. Andrew made some vague remark, wondering at the spite of fate, then forgot her utterly. Chapman had whispered to him that the cottagers were coming.

He leaned eagerly over the rail. A number of buxom dames, accompanied by slender girls, were filing in. Some of the old women were in white satin, with many jewels on their platitudinous bosoms. The slim sisterhood, with their deerlike movements, their curried hair arranged to simulate a walnut on the crown of their little heads, their tiny waists and white necks and arms, riveted Andrew's gaze as ever. Some looked like Easter lilies in their pure white gowns, others like delicate orchids. One beautiful young woman, evidently a matron, wore a gown of black gauze, with a row of sparkling crescents, stars, and clusters, about the low line of the corsage.

'Isn't she lovely?' whispered Miss Leslie. '*She* got a French Duke. But she deserved her luck. She's sweet.'

All were very *décolletée*.

'Reminds one of the days when slaves were put up on sale at the mart, not far from this very spot,' murmured Chapman.

One sprightly matron entered with an imperious air, and was immediately surrounded.

'Who's she?' enquired Andrew, scornfully. 'Why, her frock and gloves are soiled, and her hair's dyed.'

'Oh, she's out of sight, my boy! Once in a while they do look like that. She's going to lead things this summer. Wish she'd hurry up!' Then he named a number of people to Webb.

The band on the platform facing the triple row of seats at the far end began a waltz. Most of the men were elderly and well preserved. They danced with the girls. The half-dozen youths improved their chances by assiduous attentions to the unwieldy dames. Andrew thought that his princesses danced very badly. Many of them were taller than the men, and looked about to go head first over the shoulders whose support they seemed to disdain. The little ones bounded like rubber balls. The old women formed groups and gossiped. A number sat about a plethoric lady, whose diamonds made her look like a crystal chandelier. Chapman informed Webb that she was a duchess.

'You see that fellow over there!' he exclaimed, suddenly, indicating with the point of his lead-pencil a young man with a vulgar, vacuous face and a clumsy assumption of the grand air; 'well, he was nobody a year ago – a distant connection of the Webbs; but they never recognised his existence until he came into some money. Then they took him up, and now he's out of sight. It's too bad you didn't happen to be that kind of Webb. You look a long sight more of a gentleman than he does.'

'Are any of the Webbs here?' asked Andrew, choking with bitterness.

'There's the old girl over there. Regular old ice-chest.'

'Is – is – Schuyler Churchill Webb here?'

'He's just come in. He is talking to the duchess – the French one.'

Andrew gazed with dull hatred at the plain amiable-looking young man, whose air of indefinable elegance seemed to reach forth and smite him in the face. The gulf, which had been a gradually widening rift, seemed suddenly to yawn.

'Well, I must go,' said Chapman. 'I have to get my stuff off, you know. Will see you in the morning.'

As he left, Miss Leslie renewed her pleasantries, hoping that Andrew would ask her to go down and dance. She was terribly afraid of the great folk, poor little soul, but she felt that this strong self-reliant young man would protect her. Andrew excused himself in a few moments, however, and went downstairs. He had bought the right to be in the same room with those people, and he would claim it.

The treble row of seats was evidently reserved for strangers; no cottagers were at that end of the room. They sat about the other three sides with an air of being on their own ground. Andrew walked resolutely into the room, and took possession of one of the chairs reserved for his kind. He had only three or four neighbours; most of the tourists had gone upstairs, and were darkly surveying the scene. There were no decorations, but the dowagers were a jewelled dado, the girls an animated bed of blossoms.

7

For one hour Andrew sat there, and at its end he comprehended why the cottagers did not concern themselves about the tickets sold. Not one icy glance had been directed at the treble row of seats, not one enquiring stare bent upon the occasional tourist-couple who summoned courage to take a whirl. He and his companions might have been invisible intruders on a foreign planet, for all the notice the elect took of them. There was nothing overt, nothing unkind, but the stranger was as effectually frozen out as if he had fled before a battery of lorgnettes. The cottagers were like one large family. There was no more reserve among the young people than if they had been a party of happy well-trained schoolchildren. What wonder that the stranger within their gates felt his remoteness! During the 'Lancers' they almost romped. They might have been on the lawn of one of their own cottages, and these outsiders hanging on the fence. To any and all without their world they were unaffectedly oblivious.

At the end of the hour Andrew rose heavily and left his seat. His face was grey, his knees shook a little. He understood.

*   *   *

But his cup of bitterness was not yet full. As he made his way down the passage behind one of the rows of chairs reserved for the cottagers, he beheld a girl who had just entered. He stood still and stared at her, wondering that he had ever thought other women beautiful. If those he had worshipped were princesses, this was a goddess. Only New York could give her that nameless distinction, so curiously unlike the graceful breeding of older lands – the difference between the hothouse orchid and the lily of ancient parks. This girl's figure was more Junoesque than was usual with her kind, her waist larger. She was very tall. Her carriage was one of regal simplicity, as if she were wont to walk on stars. Her shining brown hair was gathered into a knot at the base of her classic head. Her brow and chin and throat were perfect in their modelling. Her skin, of a marvellous whiteness, seemed to shed a light of its own; one might surely examine it with a microscope and find no flaw. Her mouth and nose were irregular, but her large blue-grey eyes shone triumphant, and she had beautiful ears. She wore a simple gown of pale blue organdie, clinging to her faultless figure, even at the throat and wrists. At her right was the new-found relative of the Webbs, half a head too short to reach that exquisite ear with his mumblings. About her were several other men.

Andrew's capacity for love may not have been very profound, but he loved this woman at once and finally. It was a love that would have delighted the cynical Schopenhauer and the philosophical Darwin. The instinct of selection had never been more spontaneously and unerringly exercised. He was conscious of neither passion nor senti-ment, however. She hovered in his visions as a companion at great functions – his possession whom all the world would envy. It was not so much she he loved as what she represented.

His attention was momentarily distracted by the remarkable an-tics of an elderly man. This person was bowing and genuflecting before the goddess, rolling his eyes upward, throwing out his hands, clasping and wringing them – a pantomime of speechless admiration. To Andrew he looked like an elderly billygoat with a thorn in its hoof. The goddess looked down upon him with an expression of goodnatured contempt. The men applauded heartily. Andrew once more riveted his gaze on the face which had completed his undoing. In a moment the girl's clear eyes met his, then moved past as in-differently as if she had gazed upon space. Andrew turned, forgetting his hat, and almost ran from the house, down the street, and up the stairs to his apartment. He flung himself into a chair, buried his face in his hands, and groaned aloud. The hopelessness of his case surged through his brain with pitiless reiteration. He might as well attempt to fly to one of the cold stars above his casement as to besiege the society of New York. There was literally no human being out of earth's millions to give him the line that would pass him through those open invincible portals. Had he been a baboon from Central Africa, his chances would have been better; he would have compelled their attention for a moment.

There were heavy *portières* over his door; no-one could hear his groans, and he afforded himself that measure of relief. The tears ran down his cheeks; he twisted his strong hands together. Those whose hearts have been convulsed by the bitterness of love, by the loss of children, by the downfall of great hopes, may read with scorn this suffering of a snob. It may seem a mean and trivial emotion. But he has had scant opportunity to study his kind who knows nothing of the power of the snob to suffer. An artist may toil on unrecognised, yet with the deep delight of his art as compensation. A man in public life may be stung with a thousand bitter defeats, but he has the joy of the fight, the self-respect of legitimate ambition. But for the repeated defeats of even the successful snob, what compensation? Step by step he climbs, to find another still to mount, each bristling with obstacles, to which he yields the shreds and patches of his self-respect. The bitter knowledge that he is on tolerance is ever with him – that no matter how high he rises, he can never reach his goal, for at the goal are only those who have never known the need to strive. 'Tis a constant battle for a soap-bubble, an ambition without soul.

And Andrew? He had not even planted his foot on the first step. For five years he had lived in a fool's paradise, a corroding dream. There was literally nothing else on earth that he wanted. His money had come to him as the very irony of Fate. It could not give him the one thing he wished, and he had no other use for it. His dream was over. He felt like an aged man set free from an asylum for the demented after a period of incarceration which had devoured the good years of his life. He looked at what still seemed wealth to him as such a man would look at all the joys of light and liberty and taste, offered to his paralysed senses.

When the sun rose it shone down with an air of personal sympathy upon the fleet of white yachts in the bay, upon the grand old avenues, upon the relics of an historic past no cottager ever thinks of, upon the splendid houses of those who have made Newport's younger fame. And it straggled through one pair of heavy curtains and gleamed upon the white face of a young man who had joined the ranks of those that proclaim the world their conqueror.

CROWNED WITH ONE CREST

Crowned with One Crest

People were beginning to wonder if an American, having captured a title and worn it for five years, would renounce it for mere good looks and brains; in other words, if Lady Carnath, formerly Miss Edith Ingoldsby, of Washington, and still earlier – before her father had found leisure to crown a triumphant financial career with the patriotic labours of a United States Senator – of Boone, Iowa, would marry Butler Hedworth, M.P., a gentleman of some fortune and irreproachable lineage who had already made himself known on the floor of the House, but was not so much as heir-presumptive to a title. So many American maidens had placidly stood by while their mammas 'arranged' a marriage between their gold-banked selves and the impecunious scion of an historical house, that the English, when forced to admit them well-bred, found solace in the belief that these disgustingly rich and handsome girls were without heart.

Nevertheless, Lady Carnath, who had worn her weeds but a year, permitted Butler Hedworth to pay her attentions so pronounced that her world was mildly betting on his possible acceptance as husband or lover. It was argued that during the life of Lord Carnath his wife's demeanour had been above comment, but a cynic remarked that women had all sorts of odd ideals; and was widely quoted.

Edith Ingoldsby had bought her Earl and paid a high price for him; nevertheless she had liked him better than any man but one that she had ever known, and they had been the best of friends. When she met him she was in the agonies of her only passion, and had clutched the first opportunity to bury alive the love that was destroying her beauty and her interest in life.

The passion had lingered for a time, then gone the way of all passions unfed by a monotonous environment and too much leisure. She found it very interesting to be an English countess. For a while she had the impression of playing a part in a modern historical drama; but before long she realised, with true American adaptability, that her new life was but the living chapters of a book whose earlier parts had been serial instalments of retiring memory. Her great wealth, her beauty, her piquant dashing thoroughbred manner, her husband's popularity and title, created for her a position that would have closed any wound not irritated by domestic unhappiness; and this canker was not in her rose. When Carnath died she mourned him sincerely, but not too profoundly to anticipate pleasurably the end of the weeded year. When she met Hedworth she was as free of fancy and of heart as if she had but stepped from a convent.

'Yes, I was in love once – ' she admitted to him one evening as they sat alone. She blushed as she tripped at the word 'before'. Hedworth had made no declaration as yet; they were still playing with electricity, and content with sparks. 'At least, I thought I was. All girls have their love freaks. I had had several – when I was in my teens. This seemed more serious, the *grande passion* – because there was an obstacle: he was married. If he had been free, if there had been no barrier between myself and what I wanted, I think it would have been quite different. You see, I had had my own way so long that the situation, combined, of course, with the man himself – who was very magnetic – fascinated me; and I let myself go, to see what it would be like to long for something I could not have. I suppose it was my imagination that was at work principally; but I ended by believing myself frantically in love with him.'

Hedworth stood up as she paused, and leaned against the mantel, looking down at her. They were in her boudoir, a yellow satin room that looked like a large jewel-casket. Lady Carnath's long slender round figure betrayed its perfections in a gown of black chiffon; on her white neck and arms and in her black hair were many diamonds; she had dressed for the opera, then given the evening to Hedworth. Her dark face was delicately modelled; the mouth and chin were very firm, but the lips were full and red. The eyes in repose were a trifle languid, in animation mutable and brilliant. The brows were finely pencilled, and the soft dark hair, brushed back from a low forehead, added to the general distinction of her appearance. Hedworth studied her face as he had studied it many times.

'Well?' he asked. He had an abrupt voice, suggestive of temper, and the haughty bearing which is the chief attraction of Englishmen for American women. His face was as well chiselled as the average of his kind, but lacked the national repose. The eyes were very clever, the features mobile; the tenacity and strength of his nature were indicated in the lower part of his face and in the powerful yet supple build of the man.

'Well, what?'

'What sort of a man was this Johnny?'

'Oh, I am not very good at describing people – quite different from you – much lighter – '

'I don't care what he looked like. A man only looks to a woman who is in love with him as she imagines he looks. Was he in love with you?'

'Yes, of course he was.'

'Did he tell you so?'

The delicate red in Lady Carnath's dark cheek deepened. 'Yes. He did.'

'Did you tell him that you loved him?'

'Yes.'

'What did he do?'

'I don't know that you have any right to be so curious.'

'Of course you need not answer if you don't wish. Did he kiss you?'

'Yes, he did, if you want to know. We had a tremendous scene. I went into high tragics, and, I suppose, bored the poor man dreadfully.'

'He was much more matter-of-fact, I suppose?'

'Yes – he was.'

'Where did this scene take place?'

'In the drawing-room one afternoon when he had walked home with me from a tea.'

'What happened the next time you met him?'

'I never saw him again – that is, alone.'

Hedworth's face and tone changed suddenly. Both softened. 'Why not?'

She raised her head from the back of the sofa and lifted her chin defiantly. 'I did not dare – if you will know. Carnath came along shortly after, and I took him as soon as he offered himself. Why do you look so pleased? The one was as bad as the other, only in the course I took there was no scandal.'

'Which is the point. Scandal and snubs and vulgar insinuation in print and out of it would have demoralised you. How do you feel towards this man now? If he were free and came for you would you marry him?'

She shook her head, and looked up at him, smiling and blushing again. 'He is no more to me than one of the book-heroes I used to fancy myself in love with.'

'Why didn't he get a divorce and marry you? I thought anyone could get a divorce in the States.'

'You English people know so much about the United States! You are willing to believe anything and to know nothing. I really think you feel that your dignity would be compromised if you knew as much about America as we know about Europe. Your attitude is like that of old people to a new invention which is too remarkable for their powers of appreciation, so they take refuge in disdain.'

He smiled, as he always did when her patriotism flamed. 'You haven't answered my question.'

'What? – Oh, divorce. If a man has a good wife, no matter how uncongenial, he can't get rid of her unless he is a brute; and I didn't happen to like that sort of man.'

'Like? I thought you said just now that you loved him.'

'I don't think now that I did. I explained that a while ago.'

'Why have you changed your mind?'

'I never knew a man to ask so many questions.'

But before he left her he knew.

*   *   *

Edith anticipated pleasurably the sensation her engagement would make, but did not announce it at once. She had a certain feminine secretiveness which made her doubly enjoy a happiness undiluted by publicity; moreover, some further deference was due to Carnath. She was very happy, the more so as she had believed until a short while ago that her strong temperamental possibilities were vaulted in her nature's little churchyard. 'Our hearts after first love are like our dead,' she thought; 'they sleep until the hour of resurrection.' Hedworth dominated her, had taken her love rather than asked for it, and, although he was jealous and exacting, she was haunted by the traditions of man's mutability, and studied her resources as it had never occurred to her to study them before. She found that the outer envelopes of her personality could be made to shift with kaleidoscopic brilliancy, and except when Hedworth needed repose – she had much tact – she treated him to these many moods in turn. It is possible that she added to her fascination, but, having won him without effort, she might have rested on her laurels. He was deeply in love with her, and worried himself with presentiments of what might happen before she would consent to name the wedding-day. Both being children of worldly wisdom, however, they harlequined their misgivings and were happy when together.

Fortunately for both, she was heavy-laden with femininity, and was content to give all, and receive the little that man in the nature of his life and inherited particles has to offer. She was satisfied to be adored, desired, mentally appreciated. If his ego was always paramount, his spiritual demands so imperious that he appropriated the full measure of sympathy and comprehension that Nature has let loose for man and woman, not caring to know anything of her beyond the fact that she was the one woman in the world in whom he saw no fault, she was satisfied to have it so. She was a clever woman, but not too clever; and their chances of happiness were good.

And then a strange thing happened to her.

Hedworth was called to Switzerland by his mother, who fell ill. His parting with Edith occupied several hours, and during the three or four days following, his affianced protested that she was inconsolable. But his letters were frequent and characteristic, and she began to enjoy the new phase of their intercourse: the excitement of waiting for the post, the delight which the first glimpse of the envelope on her breakfast-tray gave her, the novelty of receiving a fragment of him daily, which her imagination could expand into his hourly life and thoughts. The season was over, and she had little else to do. She expected him back at any moment, and preferred to await his arrival in town.

One evening she was sitting in her bedroom thinking of him. The night was hot and the windows were open. It was very late. She had been staring down upon the dark mass of tree-tops in the Park, recapitulating, phase by phase, the growth of her feeling for Hedworth. Suddenly it occurred to her that it bore a strong racial resemblance to her first passion, and, being too intelligent to have escaped the habit of analysis, she dug up the old love and dissected it. It had been better preserved than she would have thought, for it did not offend her sense; and she gave an hour to the office. She went back to her first moment of conscious interest in the hero of her tragedy, galvanised the thrill she had felt when he entered her presence, her restlessness and doubt and jealousy when he was away, or appeared to neglect her; the recognition that she was in the hard grasp of a passion in which she had had little faith; the sweetness and terror of it, the keen delight in the sense of danger. There had been weeks of companionship before he had defined their position; it occurred to her now that he had managed her with the skill and coolness of a man who understood women and could keep his head, even while quickened with all that he inspired. She also recalled, her lips curling into a cynical grin, that she had felt the same promptings for spiritual abandonment, of high desire to help this man where he was weak, to restore some of his lost ideals, or to replace them with better; to root out the weeds which she recognised in his nature, and to coax the choked bulbs of those fairer flowers which may have been there before he and the world knew each other too well. Then she relived the days and nights of torment when she had walked the floor wringing her hands, barely eating and sleeping. She recalled that she had even beaten the walls and flung herself against them.

The procession was startlingly familiar and fresh of lineament; even the moments of rapture, whose memory is soonest to fade, and the fitful solace she had found, in those last days, imagining what might have been.

She got up and walked about the room, half amused, half appalled. 'What does it mean?' she thought. 'Is it that there is an impalpable entity in this world for me, and that part of it is in one man and part in another? Is the man who has the larger share the one I really love? Is that the explanation of loving a second time? It certainly is very like – ridiculously like.'

She turned her thoughts to Hedworth, but they swung aside and pointed straight to the other man. She half expected to see his ghost framed in the dark window, he seemed so close. She found herself living the past again and again, instinct with its sensations. He had had much in his life to cark and harrow, and the old sympathy and tenderness vibrated aloud, and little out of tune. She wondered what had become of him, what he was doing at the moment. She did not believe that he had loved any woman since; he had nearly exhausted his capacity for loving when he met her.

And at the same time she was distinctly conscious that if the two men stood before her she should spring to Hedworth. Nevertheless, when she conjured his image, the shadowy figure of the other man stood behind, looking over Hedworth's shoulder, with the half-cynical smile which had only left his mouth when he had told her, with white face whose muscles were free of his will for the moment, that he loved her.

'Is it the old love that is demanding its rights, not the man?' she thought. 'Is it true, then, that all we women want is love, and that it is as welcome in one attractive frame as another? That it is not Hedworth I love, but what he gives me? Now that I even suspect this, can I be happy? Will that ghost always look over his shoulder?'

She was a woman of sound practical sense, and had no intention of risking her happiness by falling a victim to her imagination. She pressed the electric button and wrote a letter to her former lover – a friendly letter, without sentimental allusion, asking for news of him. The sight of the handwriting that once had thrilled her, as well as the nature of his reply, would at least bring her to some sort of mental climax. Moreover, he might be dead. It might be spiritual influence that had handled her imagination. She was not a superstitious woman; she was merely wise enough to know that she knew nothing, and that it was folly to disbelieve anything.

Hedworth did not return for three weeks. During that time it seemed to her that her brain was an amphitheatre in which the two men were constantly wrestling. She never saw one without the other. When Hedworth mastered for the moment she was reminded that he was merely playing a familiar tune on her soul-keys. She felt for the man who had first touched those keys a persistent tenderness, and during the last days watched restlessly for his letter. But she felt no desire whatever to see him again. For Hedworth she longed increasingly.

Hedworth returned. The other man vanished.

* * *

She announced the engagement. They had been invited to the same houses for the autumn. Necessarily they saw little of each other, and planned to meet in the less-frequented rooms and in the woods. At first they enjoyed this new experience; but when they found themselves in a large party that seemed to pervade every corner of the house and grounds at once, and two days had passed without an interview of five minutes' duration, Hedworth walked up to her – she was alone for the moment – and said: 'Four weeks from today we marry.'

She gave a little gasp, but made no protest.

'I have had enough of dawdling and sentimentalising. We will marry at your place in Sussex on the second of October.'

'Very well,' she said.

Shortly after she went to Paris to confer with the talent that should enhance her loveliness, then paid Mrs Hedworth a visit in Switzerland. Hedworth met her there, and his mother saw little of her guests. Edith returned to England alone. Hedworth was to follow at the end of the week, and spend the few remaining days of his bachelorhood at the house of a friend whose estate adjoined the one Lady Carnath had bought not long after her husband's death.

Several days after her return she was sitting at her dressing-table when a letter was handed her bearing the Washington postmark. Her maid was devising a new coiffure, and she was grumbling at the result. She glanced at the handwriting, pushed the letter aside, and commanded the maid to arrange her hair in the simple fashion that suited her best. After the woman had fixed the last pin, Edith critically examined her profile in the triple mirror; then thrust out a thin little foot to be divested of its mule and shod in a slipper that had arrived that morning from Paris: she expected people to tea. While the maid was on her knees Edith bethought herself of the letter and read it:

> DEAR LADY CARNATH – I have been in Canada all summer. No letters were forwarded. I find yours here at the Metropolitan. Thanks, I am well. Life is the same with me. I eat and drink and wither. But you are a memory to be thankful for, and I have never tried to forget you. I was glad to learn through Tower, whom I met in Montreal, that you were well and happy. I wish I may never hear otherwise.

Then followed several pages of news of her old friends.

'Poor fellow!' thought Edith with a sigh. 'But I doubt if any woman or any circumstances would ever make a man like that happy. There are those wretched people, and I am not half dressed!'

Nevertheless, he again took his stand in her brain and elbowed Hedworth – whose concrete part was still detained in Switzerland. She did not answer the letter at once; it was not an easy letter to answer. But it haunted her; and finally she sat down at her desk and bit the end of her penholder.

She sat staring before her, the man in complete possession. And gradually the colour left her face. If this old love, which her mind and senses had corporealised, refused to abdicate, had she any right to marry Hedworth? Now that she had unlocked this ghost, might not she find it at her side whenever her husband was absent, reminding her that she was a sort of mental bigamist? Carnath had no part in her dilemma; she barely recalled his episode.

She was as positive as she had been when the past unrolled itself that she had no wish to see the first man again; that did he stand before her his power would vanish. He was a back number –

a fatal position to occupy in the imagination of a vital and world-living woman.

'Is it all that he awakened, made known to me, represented, that arises in resentment? Or is it that the soul only gives itself once, acknowledges only one mate? The mind and body, perhaps, obey the demand for companionship again. The soul in its loneliness endeavours to accompany these comrades, but finds itself linked to the mate of the past. Probably when a woman marries a man she does not love, the soul, having no demand made upon it, abstracts itself, sleeps. It is when a mate to whom it might wholly have given itself appears that, in its isolation and desolation, it clamours for its wedded part.'

Her teeth indented the nib of her penholder. 'Was ever a woman in such a predicament before? So illusionary and yet so ridiculously actual! Shall I send Hedworth away and sit down with this phantom through life? I understand that some women get their happiness out of just that sort of thing. Then when I forget Hedworth would I forget *him*? Is passion needed to set the soul free? Until Hedworth made me feel awakened womanhood personified, I had not thought of this man for years, not even during the year of my mourning, when I was rather bored. What am I to do? I can't fling my life away. I am not a morbid idiot. But I can't marry one man if what I feel for him is simply the galvanising of a corpse. Hedworth ought to be taken ill and his life despaired of. That is the way things would work out in a novel.'

Her face grew whiter still. She had experienced another mental shock. For the first time she realised that no woman could suffer twice as she had suffered five years ago. That at least was all the other man's. Her capacity for pain had been blunted, two-thirds exhausted. If Hedworth left her, died, she might regret him, long to have him back; but the ghost of that abandon of grief, that racking of every sense, that groping in an abyss while a voiceless something within her raved and shrieked, resolved itself into a finger of fire, which wrote Hedworth's inferior position.

'What shall I do? What shall I do?' She dipped the pen into the ink and put it to the paper. At least, for the moment, she could write a friendly note to this man, convey tactful sympathy, little good as it would do him. The letter must be answered.

She heard a step on the gravel beneath her open window. She sprang to her feet, the blood rushing to her hair. She ran to the window and leaned out, smiling and trembling. Hedworth's eyes flashed upward to hers. She was, it must be admitted, a product of that undulating and alluring plain we call 'the world', not of those heights where the few who have scaled them live alone.

DEATH AND THE WOMAN

Death and the Woman

Her husband was dying, and she was alone with him. Nothing could exceed the desolation of her surroundings. She and the man who was going from her were in the third-floor-back of a New York boarding-house. It was summer, and the other boarders were in the country; all the servants except the cook had been dismissed, and she, when not working, slept profoundly on the fifth floor. The landlady also was out of town on a brief holiday.

The window was open to admit the thick unstirring air; no sound rose from the row of long narrow yards, nor from the tall deep houses annexed. The latter deadened the rattle of the streets. At intervals the distant elevated lumbered protestingly along, its grunts and screams muffled by the hot suspended ocean.

She sat there plunged in the profoundest grief that can come to the human soul, for in all other agony hope flickers, however forlornly. She gazed dully at the unconscious breathing form of the man who had been friend, and companion, and lover, during five years of youth too vigorous and hopeful to be warped by uneven fortune. It was wasted by disease; the face was shrunken; the night-garment hung loosely about a body which had never been disfigured by flesh, but had been muscular with exercise and full-blooded with health. She was glad that the body was changed; glad that its beauty, too, had gone some other-where than into the coffin. She had loved his hands as apart from himself; loved their strong warm magnetism. They lay limp and yellow on the quilt: she knew that they were already cold, and that moisture was gathering on them. For a moment something convulsed within her. *They* had gone too. She repeated the words twice, and, after them, '*forever*'. And the while the sweetness of their pressure came back to her.

She leaned suddenly over him. HE was in there still, somewhere. *Where?* If he had not ceased to breathe, the Ego, the Soul, the Personality was still in the sodden clay which had shaped to give it speech. Why could it not manifest itself to her? Was it still conscious in there, unable to project itself through the disintegrating matter which was the only medium its Creator had vouchsafed it? Did it struggle there, seeing her agony, sharing it, longing for the complete disintegration which should put an end to its torment? She called his name, she even shook him slightly, mad to tear the body apart and find her mate, yet even in that tortured moment realising that violence would hasten his going.

The dying man took no notice of her, and she opened his gown and put her cheek to his heart, calling him again. There had never been more perfect union; how could the bond still be so strong if he were not at the other end of it? He was there, her other part; until dead he must be living. There was no intermediate state. Why should he be as entombed and unresponding as if the screws were in the lid? But the faintly beating heart did not quicken beneath her lips. She extended her arms suddenly, describing eccentric lines, above, about him, rapidly opening and closing her hands as if to clutch some escaping object; then sprang to her feet, and went to the window. She feared insanity. She had asked to be left alone with her dying husband, and she did not wish to lose her reason and shriek a crowd of people about her.

The green plots in the yards were not apparent, she noticed. Something heavy, like a pall, rested upon them. Then she understood that the day was over and that night was coming.

She returned swiftly to the bedside, wondering if she had remained away hours or seconds, and if he were dead. His face was still discernible, and Death had not relaxed it. She laid her own against it, then withdrew it with shuddering flesh, her teeth smiting each other as if an icy wind had passed.

She let herself fall back in the chair, clasping her hands against her heart, watching with expanding eyes the white sculptured face which, in the glittering dark, was becoming less defined of outline. Did she light the gas it would draw mosquitoes, and she could not shut from him the little air he must be mechanically grateful for. And she did not want to see the opening eye – the falling jaw.

Her vision became so fixed that at length she saw nothing, and closed her eyes and waited for the moisture to rise and relieve the strain. When she opened them his face had disappeared; the humid waves above the house-tops put out even the light of the stars, and night was come.

Fearfully, she approached her ear to his lips; he still breathed. She made a motion to kiss him, then threw herself back in a quiver of agony – they were not the lips she had known, and she would have nothing less.

His breathing was so faint that in her half-reclining position she could not hear it, could not be aware of the moment of his death. She extended her arm resolutely and laid her hand on his heart. Not only must she feel his going, but, so strong had been the comradeship between them, it was a matter of loving honour to stand by him to the last.

She sat there in the hot heavy night, pressing her hand hard against the ebbing heart of the unseen, and awaited Death. Suddenly an odd fancy possessed her. Where was Death? Why was he tarrying? Who was detaining him? From what quarter would he come? He was taking his leisure, drawing near with footsteps as measured as those of men keeping time to a funeral march. By a wayward deflection she thought of the slow music that was always turned on in the theatre when the heroine was about to appear, or something eventful to happen. She had always thought that sort of thing ridiculous and inartistic. So had He.

She drew her brows together angrily, wondering at her levity, and pressed her relaxed palm against the heart it kept guard over. For a moment the sweat stood on her face; then the pent-up breath burst from her lungs. He still lived.

Once more the fancy wantoned above the stunned heart. Death – *where* was he? What a curious experience: to be sitting alone in a big house – she knew that the cook had stolen out – waiting for Death to come and snatch her husband from her. No; he would not snatch, he would steal upon his prey as noiselessly as the approach of Sin to Innocence – an invisible, unfair, sneaking enemy, with whom no man's strength could grapple. If he would only come like a man, and take his chances like a man! Women had been known to reach the hearts of giants with the dagger's point. But he would creep upon her.

She gave an exclamation of horror. Something was creeping over the window-sill. Her limbs palsied, but she struggled to her feet and looked back, her eyes dragged about against her own volition. Two small green stars glared menacingly at her just above the sill; then the cat possessing them leaped downward, and the stars disappeared.

She realised that she was horribly frightened. 'Is it possible?' she thought. 'Am I afraid of Death, and of Death that has not yet come? I have always been rather a brave woman; *He* used to call me heroic; but then with him it was impossible to fear anything. And

I begged them to leave me alone with him as the last of earthly boons. Oh, shame!'

But she was still quaking as she resumed her seat, and laid her hand again on his heart. She wished that she had asked Mary to sit outside the door; there was no bell in the room. To call would be worse than desecrating the house of God, and she would not leave him for one moment. To return and find him dead – gone alone!

Her knees smote each other. It was idle to deny it; she was in a state of unreasoning terror. Her eyes rolled apprehensively about; she wondered if she should see It when It came; wondered how far off It was now. Not very far; the heart was barely pulsing. She had heard of the power of the corpse to drive brave men to frenzy, and had wondered, having no morbid horror of the dead. But this! To wait – and wait – and wait – perhaps for hours – past the midnight – on to the small hours – while that awful, determined, leisurely Something stole nearer and nearer.

She bent to him who had been her protector with a spasm of anger. Where was the indomitable spirit that had held her all these years with such strong and loving clasp? How could he leave her? How could he desert her? Her head fell back and moved restlessly against the cushion; moaning with the agony of loss, she recalled him as he had been. Then fear once more took possession of her, and she sat erect, rigid, breathless, awaiting the approach of Death.

Suddenly, far down in the house, on the first floor, her strained hearing took note of a sound – a wary, muffled sound, as if someone were creeping up the stair, fearful of being heard. Slowly! It seemed to count a hundred between the laying down of each foot. She gave a hysterical gasp. Where was the slow music?

Her face, her body, were wet – as if a wave of death-sweat had broken over them. There was a stiff feeling at the roots of her hair; she wondered if it were really standing erect. But she could not raise her hand to ascertain. Possibly it was only the colouring matter freezing and bleaching. Her muscles were flabby, her nerves twitched helplessly.

She knew that it was Death who was coming to her through the silent deserted house; knew that it was the sensitive ear of her intelligence that heard him, not the dull, coarse-grained ear of the body.

He toiled up the stair painfully, as if he were old and tired with much work. But how could he afford to loiter, with all the work he had to do? Every minute, every second, he must be in demand to hook his cold, hard finger about a soul struggling to escape from its putrefying tenement. But probably he had his emissaries, his minions: for only those worthy of the honour did he come in person.

He reached the first landing and crept like a cat down the hall to the next stair, then crawled slowly up as before. Light as the footfalls were, they were squarely planted, unfaltering; slow, they never halted.

Mechanically she pressed her jerking hand closer against the heart; its beats were almost done. They would finish, she calculated, just as those footfalls paused beside the bed.

She was no longer a human being; she was an Intelligence and an EAR. Not a sound came from without, even the Elevated appeared to be temporarily off duty; but inside the big quiet house that footfall was waxing louder, louder, until iron feet crashed on iron stairs and echo thundered.

She had counted the steps – one – two – three – irritated beyond endurance at the long deliberate pauses between. As they climbed and clanged with slow precision she continued to count, audibly and with equal precision, noting their hollow reverberation. How many steps had the stair? She wished she knew. No need! The colossal trampling announced the lessening distance in an increasing volume of sound not to be misunderstood. It turned the curve; it reached the landing; it advanced – slowly – down the hall; it paused before her door. Then knuckles of iron shook the frail panels. Her nerveless tongue gave no invitation. The knocking became more imperious; the very walls vibrated. The handle turned, swiftly and firmly. With a wild instinctive movement she flung herself into the arms of her husband.

* * *

When Mary opened the door and entered the room she found a dead woman lying across a dead man.

A PROLOGUE
[to an unwritten play]

A Prologue

[to an unwritten play]

Characters: JAMES HAMILTON, MARY FAWCETT, RACHAEL LAVINE, two slaves. Place: Nevis, British West Indies. Time: The month of April, 1756.

[A large room, with open windows, to which are attached heavy inside wooden shutters furnished with iron bars. Beyond the windows are seen masses of tropical trees and foliage, green and more brilliantly hued, filled with screaming birds and monkeys. In the court is a fountain. The house is half-way up the mountain, and between the trees is a glint of the sea. The room is severely simple. There are no curtains, carpets, nor upholstered furniture; but there are two handsome pieces of mahogany, a bookcase full of books bound in old calf, a table on which are tropical fruits and cooling drinks in earthen jugs, one or two palm trees, and Caribbean pottery on shelves. In one corner is a harp.

In the distance is heard a loud menacing roar. The sky is covered with racing clouds. Suffusing everything is a livid light.

Mistress Fawcett is leaning on her crutch, looking through one of the windows. Two slaves are crouching on the floor. All are in an intense attitude, listening. Suddenly there is heard the quick loud firing of cannon, four guns in rapid succession. The negroes shriek and crouch lower as if they would insinuate their trembling bodies through the floor. Mistress Fawcett hastily closes the window by which she is standing, swings to and bars its shutters. Immediately after may be heard the sound, gradually diminishing in the distance, of a long line of windows slammed and barred. Mistress Fawcett attempts to move the shutters of the other window, but the hinges are rusty and defy her feeble strength.]

MISTRESS FAWCETT *[to the slaves]*. Come here. Close this window. Did you not hear the guns? A hurricane is upon us.

THE SLAVES *[crouching lower and wailing almost unintelligibly]*. Oh, mistress, save us! Send for oby doctor!

MISTRESS FAWCETT. To strangle you with a horsehair pie! Your obeah charlatans are grovelling in their cellars. Only our courage and our two hands can save us today. Come! [*beating the floor with her crutch*] A hundred man slaves on the estate, and not one to help us save the house! Are my daughter and I to do it all? Get up! [*she menaces them with her crutch*]

THE SLAVES [*not moving*]. Oh, mistress!

[*enter* RACHAEL. *She walks to the open window and looks out.*]

MISTRESS FAWCETT. Close the windows, Rachael. I cannot. And those creatures are empty skulls.

RACHAEL. In a moment.

MISTRESS FAWCETT. In a moment? Open your ears. Do you want to see the roof racing with the wind?'

RACHAEL. The hurricane is still miles away.

MISTRESS FAWCETT. Great God! How can you stand there and wait for a hurricane? Do you realise that an hour, if this old house be not strong enough, may see us struggling out in those roaring waters? These desolate afflicted Caribbees! They have tested my courage many times, and I can go through this without flinching; but I cannot stand that unnatural calm of yours.

RACHAEL. Do I seem calm? [*she closes and bars the window*] It is a fine sight. We may never have such another.

MISTRESS FAWCETT. Nor live to know.

RACHAEL [*her back is still turned, as she shakes and tests the window*]. Well, what of that? Are you so in love with life?

MISTRESS FAWCETT. Even at sixty I am in no haste to be blown out of it. And if I were twenty –

RACHAEL [*turning suddenly, and facing her mother*]. At twenty, with forty years of nothingness before you, cut off from all the joy of life, on an island in the Caribbean Sea, what then? [*she snaps her fingers*] That for the worst a hurricane can do!

MISTRESS FAWCETT [*uneasily*]. Do not let us talk of personal things today.

RACHAEL. I never felt more personal.

MISTRESS FAWCETT [*looking at her keenly*]. I believe you are excited.

RACHAEL [*she clinches her hands and brings them up sharply to her breast*]. Excited! Call it that if you like. All my life I have longed for the hurricane, and now I feel as if it were coming to me alone.

MISTRESS FAWCETT [*evasively*]. I do not always understand you, Rachel. You are a strange girl.

RACHAEL [*bursting through her assumed composure*]. Strange? Because I long to feel the mountain shaken, as I have been shaken through four terrible weeks? Because I long to hear the wind roar and shriek its derision of man, make his quaking soul forget every law he ever knew, stamp upon him, grind him to pulp –

MISTRESS FAWCETT. Hush! What are you saying? I do not know you – 'the ice-plant of the tropics', indeed! The electricity of this hurricane has bewitched you.

RACHAEL. That I will not deny. [*she laughs*] But I do deny that I am not myself, whether you recognise me or not. Which self that you have seen do you think my real one? First, the dreaming girl, in love with books, the sun, the sea, and a future that no man has written in books; then, while my scalp is still aching from my newly turned hair, I am thrust through the church doors into the arms of a brute. A year of dumb horror, and I run from his house in the night, to my one friend, the mother who –

MISTRESS FAWCETT. Not another word! I believed in him! There wasn't a mother on St Kitts who did not envy me. No-one could have imagined –

RACHAEL. No-one but a girl of sixteen, to whom no-one would listen –

MISTRESS FAWCETT. I commanded you to hush.

RACHAEL. Command the hurricane! I will speak!

MISTRESS FAWCETT. Very well, speak. It may be our last hour – who knows? [*she seats herself, sets her lips, and presses her hands hard on the handle of her crutch*]

RACHAEL. Did you think you knew me in the two years that followed, years when I was as speechless as while in bondage to John Lavine, when I crouched in the dark corners, fearing the light, the sound of every man's voice? Then health again, and normal interests, but not hope – not hope! At nineteen I had lived too long! You are sixty, and you have not the vaguest idea what that means! Then, four weeks ago –

MISTRESS FAWCETT. Ah!

RACHAEL. James Hamilton came. Ah, how unprepared I was! That I – *I* should ever look upon another man except with loathing! Sixty and twenty – perhaps somewhere between is the age of wisdom! And the law holds me fast to a man who is not fit to live! All nature awoke in me and sang the hour I met Hamilton. For the first time I loved children, and longed for them. For the first time I saw God in man. For the first time the future seemed vast, interminable, yet all too short. And if I go to this man who has made me feel great and wonderful enough to bear a demigod, a wretch can divorce and disgrace me! Oh, these four terrible weeks – ecstasy, despair – ecstasy, despair – and to the world as unblinking as a marble in a museum! Do you wonder that I welcome the hurricane, in which no man dare think of any but his puny self? For the moment I am free, and as alive, as triumphant as that great wind outside – as eager to devastate, to fight, to conquer, to live – to live – to live. What do I care for civilisation? If James Hamilton were out there among the flying trees and called to me, I would go. Hark! Listen! Is it not magnificent?

[*The hurricane is nearer and louder. The approaching roar is varied by sudden tremendous gusts, the hissing and splashing of water, the howling of negroes and dogs, the wild pealing of bells. In the room below is heard the noise of many trampling feet, slamming of windows, and smothered exclamations.*]

Mistress Fawcett. The negroes have taken refuge in the cellar – every one of them, beyond a doubt, two hundred and more! God grant they do not die of fright or suffocation. It is useless to attempt to coax them up here. These only wait until our backs are turned. Look!

[*The slaves have crawled to the door on the left. They are livid. Their tongues hang out. Rachael runs forward, seizes them by their long hair, and administers a severe shaking.*]

Rachael. Wake up! Wake up! We need your help. The windows must be watched every moment.

[*A terrible gust shakes the house. As Rachael relaxes her hold, the slaves collapse again, but clutch at her skirts, mumbling and wailing. Rachael gazes at them a moment, makes a motion as if to spurn them with her foot, then shrugs her shoulders and opens the door.*]

Rachael. Go. Die in your own way. May I be granted the same privilege some day.

[*The slaves stumble out.*]

Mistress Fawcett. I see you recognise no will but your own tonight. They are my slaves, and I had bidden them stay. But in truth they are useless; and as for you – have your little hour. I embittered too many. It may be your last. And – thank God! – Hamilton is not here.

RACHAEL [*with great agitation*]. Where is he? At sea? Riding over the mountain – far from shelter –

MISTRESS FAWCETT. Trust any man to take care of himself, let alone a Scot. No doubt he is over on St Kitts, brewing swizzle with Will Hamilton. Will's house is one of the strongest in the Caribbees. Look!

[*One of the heavy shutters has been forced open by the wind, which has shattered the outer glass. Leaves and glass fly into the room. Rachael and her mother hurl themselves against the heavy wooden blind. By exerting all their strength they succeed in fastening it again. Then they examine the other window. Mistress Fawcett sits down, panting, holding her hand to her heart.*]

RACHAEL. I will see to the other windows. [*she runs out of the room*]

MISTRESS FAWCETT. If she knew that Hamilton was on Nevis an hour before the guns were fired! As like as not he helped to fire them, for he is a guest at the Fort. If I had not commanded him to go when he came this afternoon, he would be here now. Thank heaven, no man could breast this hurricane and live! I know her! I know her – little as she thinks it! Will she continue to obey me? And after I am dead? Ah! Do I allow myself to fear aught in this hurricane, I shall never see the morning. [*she presses her hand hard against her heart, and composes herself*]

[*Rachael returns. She pours out a drink and forces her mother to take it, while her own head is erect and listening. Her nostrils dilate; one can almost see her ears quiver. The wind increases every moment in violence. In it may now be heard a peculiar monotonous rattle, the agitation of seeds in the dry pods of the 'giant' tree.*]

RACHAEL. Did you see? I had but a glimpse, but hours could not have made the picture more vivid. I could *see* the great wind. The tops of the palms are flying about like Brobdingnagian birds, their long blades darting out like infuriated tongues. I saw the oranges flung about in a great game of battledore and shuttlecock – as if the hurricane remembered to play in its fury! I saw men shrieking at the masts of a ship. Their puny lives! Why are they not glad to die so splendid a death?

MISTRESS FAWCETT. Thank God, Hamilton is not here!

RACHAEL. I tell you that, if he were, the greatest man of his time would one day call you grandam.

MISTRESS FAWCETT [*rising with energy*]. Hark ye, Rachael! Calm yourself! You have had your hour of wildness. I understand your mood – the relief, the delight to give to the storm what you cannot give to Hamilton. But enough! I can stand no more. I am old. My heart is nearly worn out. If the storm unnerves me, I am undone.

RACHAEL. Very well, mother. I will put my soul back in its coffin – if I can. This is a favourable moment. There is a lull.

MISTRESS FAWCETT [*she seats herself again*]. Come here, Rachael. [*Rachael, who has apparently calmed herself, approaches and stands beside her mother. She tenderly rearranges the old woman's hair, which fell from her cap during her struggle with the blind.*] Rachael, these hours, I repeat, may be our last on earth. This house is old. The hurricane may uproot it. Like you, I am not afraid to die. Indeed, I should welcome death tonight if I could take you with me. Bitterer than any pain has been the thought of leaving you alone in the world. I am glad you have broken the silence you imposed. I never could have broken it. I ask you now to forgive me, and I acknowledge that I alone was responsible for the tragedy of your married life. That I was deceived is no excuse. I am reckoned more astute than most. I should have known that behind that white and purring exterior was a cruel and hideous voluptuary. But I had known Danes all my life, and respected them, and you were the child of my old age. I knew that I had not long to live. But I am not making excuses. I ask you humbly to forgive me.

RACHAEL. Forgive you! I have been bred in philosophy, and I have always loved you perfectly.

MISTRESS FAWCETT. Ah! I did not know. Until tonight you have been so reticent. And silent people think – think –

RACHAEL. I have thought, but never to blame you. And what is past is past. I waste no time on what cannot be undone. The soul must have its education, and part of that is to be torn up by the roots, trampled, beaten, crucified. Let me hope that, having had that course at the beginning of my life, I have had it once for all.

MISTRESS FAWCETT. There are worse things than a loveless marriage with a brute. One is to love a man you cannot marry, and be cast aside by him, while your heart is still alive with the love he has sloughed off like an old skin that has begun to chafe. And then, without friends – with children, perhaps, the world snatching at its skirts as it passes you – the uncommon and terrible disgrace of divorce. Rachael! – will you not promise me –

RACHAEL. I promise you this – in normal mood, I will think of you first. But, do I ever meet Hamilton when I feel as I do tonight, I should not think – not think, I say – not think nor care! Am I like those cattle in the cellar? Did not Nature fashion me to love and hate, to create and suffer – to feel as she does tonight?

MISTRESS FAWCETT [*with a long sigh*]. Thank heaven, Hamilton is not here! Ah!

RACHAEL. Yes, it comes again.

[*The hurricane bursts with renewed fury. The concussions are like the impact of artillery. Hail rattles on the roof. Trees and roofs crash against one another in mid-air. Suddenly the house springs and rocks. Simultaneously there is a long horrid shriek from the negroes in the cellar.*]

RACHAEL. Has Nevis been torn from her foundations?

MISTRESS FAWCETT. It was an earthquake. A hurricane tugs at the very roots of the earth. Pray heaven that the fires in Nevis are out. But we have no time to think on imaginary horrors. Look to the windows. [*as Rachael examines the windows, Mistress Fawcett thrusts her head towards the outer door, as if listening in an agony of apprehension. She raises herself from the chair, her eyes expanded, but keeps her face turned from Rachael, and says, steadily*]: I think I hear the rattle of a shutter in the dining-room. Run and see. And examine all the other windows before you return. Remember that if the wind gets in, the roof will go. [*Rachael runs out of the room. Immediately after there is a loud knocking at the front door, which is on the side of the house at present sheltered from the direct attack of the storm. Mistress Fawcett hobbles forward and secures more firmly the iron bar, making it impossible for an outsider to force his way in.*]

MISTRESS FAWCETT. Who is there?

[*A Voice without*]. It is I – James Hamilton.

MISTRESS FAWCETT. You cannot enter.

HAMILTON. Not enter? I have braved death, and worse, to come to you, knowing that you were alone. Nor would you leave a dog out on such a day.

MISTRESS FAWCETT. I would open to the most desperate criminal in the islands, but not to you. Go! Go! At once! [*she turns her head in great anxiety towards the long line of rooms where Rachael is examining the windows.*] Surely she cannot hear us; the wind is too great. [*raising her voice again*] You cannot enter. If my daughter opens the door to you, it will be after violence to me. Now will you go – or, at least, make no further sign? You are welcome to the shelter of the veranda until the hurricane veers, when you can take refuge in an outhouse.

HAMILTON. You have not an outhouse on the estate. Not one stone is upon another, except in this house. Hardly a tree is standing. If you send me away, it is to certain death.

MISTRESS FAWCETT [*in a tone of great distress*]. What shall I do? I do not wish you so ill as that. If I admit you, will you let me hide you? Promise me not to reveal yourself to Rachael?

HAMILTON. I will not promise.

[*Rachael enters. She raises her head with a quick half-comprehending motion.*]

RACHAEL. Who is out there?

MISTRESS FAWCETT [*she turns sharply, draws herself up, and places her back to the door*]. James Hamilton.

RACHAEL. Ah! [*she is about to advance quickly, when she notes the significance of her mother's face and attitude*] Let him in!

MISTRESS FAWCETT. No.

RACHAEL. It is not possible! You? Why, he must be half dead. But, of course, you are only waiting to extract a promise from me.

MISTRESS FAWCETT. Will you make it?

RACHAEL. No.

MISTRESS FAWCETT. Then he can die out there in the storm. [*Rachael laughs, and approaches her swiftly. Mistress Fawcett raises her hand warningly.*] I shall struggle with you, and you know that will mean *my* death. You may choose between us.

[*Rachael utters a cry, and covers her face with her hands. Hamilton throws himself against the door with violence, but the iron bar guards it.*]

HAMILTON. The hurricane is veering, Mistress Fawcett. Do not you *hear* the absolute stillness? In a few moments it will burst out of the west with increased fury. Unless you admit me, I shall stay here and meet it. I have crawled here, wriggled here, like a snake. It has taken me two hours to cover half a mile. I shall not crawl back. I came here to protect Rachael – to die with her, if inevitable –

MISTRESS FAWCETT. Or to ruin her life.

HAMILTON. That is done.

MISTRESS FAWCETT. True; but I can protect her from worse.

RACHAEL. Very well! You can keep him out. You cannot keep me in. I shall not struggle with you; nor will I admit anyone to your house against your will. But if you do not open that door – at once – I go out by another.

MISTRESS FAWCETT. Rachael! Do I count for nothing? I have loved you so! Is this all you have to give me in return?

RACHAEL. I know your motive – your love. I misprise neither. But if women loved their mothers better than the man of their hearts there would be the end of the race. And what is the will of either of us against Fate? Cannot you understand? Why was he permitted to reach me tonight? What man has ever lived through a hurricane before? Nature has held her breath to let him pass. Do you suppose your puny strength can hold us apart? Quick! Answer! [*she half turns towards the door leading into the next room*]

MISTRESS FAWCETT. You have conquered. But wait until I am out of this room. [*She falls heavily on her crutch, and hobbles out. Rachael holds her breath until the door closes behind her, then runs forward and lowers the bar. Hamilton enters. He is hatless. His long cape is torn and covered with leaves and mould. He closes and bars the door behind him, and Rachael, seeing him safe, and her desire so near to fulfilment, experiences a revulsion of feeling. She falls back, and hurriedly fetching a pan of coals from a corner, fires them, and mixes a punch.*]

RACHAEL [*hurriedly*]. You are cold. You are exhausted. In a moment I will give you a hot drink.

[*Hamilton, after a long look at her, throws himself into a chair by the table, and stares at the floor, his hand at his head.*]

HAMILTON. Thank you. I need it. I feel as if all the hurricane were in my head.

RACHAEL [*pouring the punch into a silver goblet*]. Drink.

HAMILTON. Gratefully! [*he raises the goblet*] I drink – to the hurricane.

RACHAEL [*she moves restlessly about, but remains on the other side of the table*]. Tell me of your journey here. I should think you would be grey and old! Ah, the colour comes back to your face! You are young again, already.

HAMILTON [*he has drained the goblet and set it on the table; he rises, and looks full at her*]. Did you doubt that I would come?

RACHAEL [*speaking lightly, and averting her eyes*]. I thought you were on St Kitts.

HAMILTON [*vehemently*]. Still I would have come. I knew the hurricane would give you to me. And out there, fighting inch by inch, the breath beaten out of my body, my arms almost torn from their sockets, maddened by the terrible confusion, I still knew that Nature was driving me to you, as she has separated us since the day I came, with her smiling, intolerable calm –

RACHAEL [*still half-frivolous under the sudden wrench from tragic despair*]. And, after that terrible experience, you still have love and romance in you! I should want a warm bed, and then – tomorrow – tomorrow – we will sit on the terrace and watch the calm old sun go down into the calm old sea, with not a thought for the torn old earth –

HAMILTON. Rachael! I did not come here to jest.

RACHAEL. I must go to my mother! She is alone! *What* have I done?

HAMILTON. Stay where you are! Do you mean that you wish you had not opened the door?

RACHAEL [*she hesitates a moment, then raises her eyes to his, and answers distinctly*]. No! [*She is leaning on the table, which she has deliberately kept between them. Hamilton throws himself into his chair, and, leaning forward, clasps her wrists with his hands.*]

HAMILTON. This hurricane is the end of all things, or the beginning.

RACHAEL [*she throws her head back, with a gesture of triumph*]. The beginning!

HAMILTON. Yes, the storm has come as a friend, not as an enemy, no matter which way – no matter which way. [*he speaks hoarsely and slowly. There is a silence, during which they stare at each other until both are breathless, and the table, under the pressure of Hamilton's arms, slowly slips aside.*]

RACHAEL. Hark!

HAMILTON. Yes; the storm returns.

[*Without further warning, the hurricane bursts out of the west with the fury of recuperated power. The house trembles. The slaves screech in the cellar. A deluge of water descends on the roof. The confusion waxes louder and louder, until it seems as if the noise alone must grind all things to dust. Hamilton thrusts aside the table, and takes Rachael violently in his arms. Her laugh of delight and triumph blends curiously with the furious noise of the hurricane.*]

TALBOT OF URSULA

Talbot of Ursula

I

The Señora as usual had written a formal little note in the morning asking John Talbot to eat his birthday dinner at the Rancho de los Olivos. Although he called on the Señora once a week the year round, she never offered him more than a glass of angelica or a cup of chocolate on any other occasion; but for his natal day she had a turkey killed, and her aged cook prepared so many hot dishes and *dulces* of the old time that Talbot was a wretched man for three days. But he would have endured misery for six rather than forego this feast, and the brief embrace of home life that accompanied it.

The Señora and the padre of the Mission were Talbot's only companions in Santa Ursula, although for political reasons he often dropped in at the saloon of the village and discussed with its polyglot customers such affairs of the day as penetrated this remote corner of California. And yet for twenty-three years he had lived in Santa Ursula, year in and year out, save for brief visits to San Francisco, Sacramento, and the Southern towns.

Why had he stayed on in this God-forsaken hole after he had become a rich man? He asked himself the question with some humour as he walked up and down the corridor of the Mission on this his fortieth birthday; and he had asked it many times.

To some souls the perfect peace, the warm drowsy beauty of the scene would have been a conclusive answer. Two friars in their brown robes passed and repassed him, reading their prayers. Beyond the arches of the corridor, abruptly below the plateau on which stood the long white Mission, was, so far as the eye was responsible, an illimitable valley, cutting the horizon on the south and west, cut by the mountains of Santa Barbara on the east. The sun was brazen in a dark-blue sky, and under its downpour the vast olive orchard which covered the valley looked like a silver sea. The glittering ripples met the blue of the horizon sharply, crinkled against the lower spurs of the mountain. As a bird that had skimmed its surface, then plunged for a moment, rose again, Talbot almost expected to see it shake bright drops from its wings. He sighed involuntarily as he reflected that in the dark caves and arbours below it was very cool, far cooler than he would be during an eight-mile ride under the midday sun of Southern California. Then he remembered that the Señora's *sala* was also dark and cool, and that part of his way lay through the cotton-woods and willows by the river; and he smiled whimsically again. He had salted his long sojourn at Santa Ursula with much philosophy.

One mountain-peak, detached from the range and within a mile of the Mission, was dense and dark with forest, broken only here and there by the boulders the earth had flung on high in her restless youth. There was but a winding trail to the top, and few had made acquaintance with it. John Talbot knew it well, and that to which it led – a lake in the very cup of the peak, so clear and bright that it reflected every needle of the dark pines embracing it.

And to the west of the Mission – past the river with its fringe of cotton-woods and willows, beyond a long dusty road which led through fields and cañon and over more than one hill – was the old adobe house of the Rancho de los Olivos.

Talbot was a practical man of business today. The olive orchard was his, the toy hotel at the end of the plateau, the land upon which had grown the rough village, with its one store, its prosperous saloon, its post-office, and several shanties of citizens not altogether estimable. He was also a man of affairs, for he had represented the district for two years at the State Legislature, and was spoken of as a future Senator. It cannot be said that the people among whom he had spent so many years of his life loved him, for he was reserved and had never been known to slap a man on the back. Moreover, it was believed that he subscribed to a San Francisco daily paper, which he did not place on file in the saloon, and that he had a large library of books in one of his rooms at the Mission. As far as the neighbours could see, the priest was the only man in the district in whom he found companionship. Nevertheless he was respected and trusted as a man must be who has never broken his word nor taken advantage of another for twenty-three years; and even those who resented the manifest antagonism of his back to the national familiarity felt that the dignity and interest of the State would be safe in his hands. Even those most in favour of rotation had concluded that it would not be a bad idea to put him in Congress for life, after the tacit fashion of the New England States. At all events they would try him in the House of Representatives for two or three terms, and then, if he satisfied their expectations and demonstrated his usefulness, they would 'work' the State and send him to the United States Senate. Santa Ursula had but one street, but its saloon was the heart of a hundred-mile radius. And it was as proud as an old don. When its leading citizen became known far and wide as 'Talbot of Ursula', a title conferred by the members of his Legislature to distinguish him from two colleagues of the same name, its pride in him knew no bounds. The local papers found it an effective headline, and the title clung to him for the rest of his life.

It was only when a newspaper interviewed Talbot after his election to the State Senate that his district learned that he was by birth an Englishman. He had emigrated with his parents at the age of fourteen, however, and as the population of his district included Germans, Irish, Swedes, Mexicans, and Italians, his nationality mattered little. Moreover, he had made his own fortune, barring the start his uncle had given him, and he was an American every inch of him. England was but a peaceful dream, a vale of the hereafter's rest set at the wrong end of life. He recalled but one incident of that time, but on that incident his whole life had hinged.

It was some years now since it had grouped itself, a tableau of grey ghosts, in his memory, but he invoked it today, although it seemed to have no place in the hot languid morning with that Southern sea hiding its bitter fruit breaking almost at the feet of this long white red-tiled Mission whose silver bells had once called hundreds of Indians to prayer. (They rang with vehemence still, but few responded.) Nevertheless the memory rose and held him.

His mother, a widow, had kept a little shop in his native village. He had gone to school since the tender age of five, and had paid more attention to his books than to the village battleground, for he grew rapidly, and was very delicate until the change to the new world made a man of him. But he loved his books, the other boys were kind to him, and altogether he was not ill-pleased with his life when one day his mother bade him put on his best clothes and come with her to a wedding. He grumbled disdainfully, for he had an interesting book in his hand; but he was used to obey his mother; he tumbled into his Sunday clothes and followed her and other dames to the old stone church at the top of the village. The daughter of the great family of the neighbourhood was to be married that morning, and all the little girls of John's acquaintance were dressed in white and had strewn flowers along the main street and the road beyond as far as the castle gates. He thought it a silly business and a sinful waste of posies; but in the churchyard he took his place in the throng with a certain feeling of curiosity.

The bride happened to be one of the beauties of her time; but it was not so much her beauty that made John stare at her with expanding eyes and mouth as she drove up in an open carriage, then walked down the long path from the gate to the church. He had seen beauty before, but never that look and air of a race far above his own, of light impertinent pride, never a lissom daintily-stepping figure, and a head carried as if it bore a star rather than a bridal wreath. He had not dreamed of anything alive resembling this, and he knew she was not an angel. After she had entered the church he drew a long breath and glanced sharply at the village beauties. They looked like coarse red apples; and, alas, his mother was of their world.

When the bride reappeared he stared hard at her again, but this time he noticed that there were similar delicate beings in her train. She was not the only one of her kind, then. The discovery filled him with amazement, which was followed by a curious sensation of hope. He broke away from his mother and ran after the carriage for nearly a mile, determined to satisfy his eager eyes as long as might be. The bride noticed him, and, smiling, tossed him a rose from her bouquet. He had that flower yet.

It was a week before he confided to his mother that when he grew up he intended to marry a lady. Mrs Talbot stared, then laughed. But when he repeated the statement a few evenings later during their familiar hour, she told him peremptorily to put such ideas out of his head, that the likes of him didn't marry ladies. And when he explained why, with the brutal directness she thought necessary, John was as depressed as a boy of fourteen can be. It was but a week later, however, that his mother, upon announcing her determination to emigrate to America, said to him: 'And perhaps you'll get that grand wish of yours. Out there I've heard say as how one body's as good as another, so if you're a good boy and make plenty of brass, you can marry a lady as well as not.' She forgot the words immediately, but John never forgot them.

Mrs Talbot died soon after their arrival in New York, and the brother who had sent for her put John to school for two years. One day he told him to pack his trunk and accompany him to California in search of gold. They bought a comfortable emigrant wagon and joined a large party about to cross the plains in quest of El Dorado. During that long momentous journey John felt like a character in a book of adventures, for they had no less than three encounters with red Indians, and two of his party were scalped. He always felt young again when he recalled that time. It was one of those episodes in life when everything was exactly as it should be.

He and his uncle remained in the San Joaquin valley for a year, and although they were not so fortunate as many others, they finally moved to San Francisco the richer by a few thousands. Here Mr Quick opened a gambling-house and saloon, and made money far more rapidly than he had done in the northern valley – where, in truth, he had lost much by night that he had panned out by day. But being a virtuous uncle, if an imperfect member of society, he soon sent John to the country to look after a ranch near the Mission of Santa Ursula. The young man never knew that this fine piece of property had been won over the gambling table from Don Roberto Ortega, one of the maddest grandees of the Californias. His grant embraced some fifty thousand acres and was bright in patches with little olive orchards. John planted with olive trees, at his own expense, the twelve thousand acres which had fallen to his uncle's share; the two men were to be partners, and the younger was to inherit the elder's share. He inherited nothing else, for his uncle married a Mexican woman who knifed him and made off with what little money had been put aside from current extravagances. But John worked hard, bought *varas* in San Francisco whenever he had any spare cash, supplied almost the entire State with olives and olive-oil, and in time became a rich man.

And his ideal? Only the Indians had driven it temporarily into the unused chambers of his memory. Not gold-mines, nor his brief taste of the wild hot life of San Francisco, nor hard work among his olive trees, nor increasing wealth and importance, had driven from his mind that desire born among the tombstones of his native village. It was the woman herself with a voice as silver as his own olive leaves, who laughed his dream to death, and left him, still handsome, strong, and lightly touched by time, a bachelor at forty.

He saw nothing of women for several years after he came to the Mission, for the one ranch house in the neighbourhood was closed, and there was no village then. He worked among his olive trees contentedly enough, spending long profitable evenings with the intellectual priests, who made him one of their family, and studying law and his favourite science, political economy. Although the boy was very handsome, with his sunburned, well-cut face and fine figure, it never occurred to the priests that the most romantic of hearts beat beneath that shrewd, accumulative brain. Of women he had never spoken, except when he had confided to his friends that he was glad to get away from the very sight of the terrible creatures of San Francisco; and that he dreamed for hours among his olive trees of the thoroughbred creature who was one day to reward his labours and make him the happiest of mortals never entered the imagination of the good padres.

He was twenty and the ranch was his when he met Delfina Carillo. Don Roberto Ortega had opportunely died before gambling away more than half of his estate, and his widow, who was delicate, left the ranch near Monterey, where they had lived for many years, and came to bake brown in the hot suns of the South. Her son, Don Enrique, came with her, and John saw him night and morning riding about the country at top speed, and sometimes clattering up to the corridor of the Mission and calling for a glass of wine. He was a magnificent caballero, slim and dark, with large melting eyes and long hair on a little head. He wore small-clothes of gaily coloured silk, with much lace on his shirt and silver on his sombrero. His long yellow botas were laced with silver, and his saddle was so loaded with the same metal that only a Californian horse could have carried it. John turned up his nose at this gorgeous apparition, and likened him to a 'play actor' and a circus rider; nevertheless, he was very curious to see something of the life of the Californian grandee, of which he had heard much and seen nothing, and when Padre Ortega, who was a cousin of the widow, told him that a large company was expected within a fortnight, and that he had asked permission to take his young friend to the ball with which the festivities would open, John began to indulge in the pleasurable anticipations of youth.

But he did not occupy the interval with dreams alone. He went to San Francisco and bought himself a wardrobe suitable for polite society. It was an American outfit, not Californian, but had John possessed the wealth of the northern valleys he could not have been induced to put himself into silk and lace.

The stage did not go to Santa Ursula, but a servant met him at a station twenty miles from home with a horse, and a cart for his trunk. He washed off the dust of three days' travel in a neighbouring creek, then jumped on his big grey mare, and started at a mild gallop for his ranch. He felt like singing his contentment with the world, for the morning was radiant, he was on one of the finest horses of the country, and he was as light of heart as a boy should be who has received a hint from fortune that he is one of the favourites. He looked forward to the social ordeal without apprehension, for by this time he had all the native American's sense of independence, he had barely heard the word 'gentleman' since his arrival in the new country, his education was all that could be desired, he was a landed proprietor, and intended to be a rich and successful man. No wonder he wanted to sing.

He had ridden some eight or ten miles, meeting no-one in that great wilderness of early California, when he suddenly drew rein and listened. He was descending into a narrow cañon on whose opposite slope the road continued to the interior; his way lay sharply to the south when he reached the narrow stream between the walls of the cañon. The sound of many voices came over the hills opposite, and the voices were light, and young, and gay. John remembered that it was time for Doña Martina's visitors to arrive, and guessed at once that he was about to fall in with one of the parties. The young Californians travelled on horseback in those days, thinking nothing of forty miles under a midsummer sun. John, who was the least self-conscious of mortals, was moved to gratitude that he wore a new suit of grey serge and had left the dust of stage travel in the creek.

The party appeared on the crest of the hill, and began the descent into the cañon. John raised his cap, and the caballeros responded with a flourish of sombreros. It would be some moments before they could meet, and John was glad to stare at the brilliant picture they made. Life suddenly seemed unreal, unmodern to him. He forgot his olive trees, and recalled the tales the priests had told him of the pleasures and magnificence of the Californian dons before the American occupation.

The caballeros were in silk, every one of them, and for variety of hue they would have put a June garden to the blush. Their linen and silver were dazzling, and the gold-coloured coats of their horses seemed a reflection of the sun. These horses had silver tails and manes, and seemed invented for the brilliant creatures who rode them. The girls were less gorgeous than the caballeros, for they wore delicate flowered gowns, and a strip of silk about their heads instead of sombreros trimmed with silver eagles. But they filled John's eye, and he forgot the caballeros. They had long black braids of hair and large dark eyes and white skins, and at that distance they all looked beautiful; but although John worshipped beauty, even in the form of olive trees and purple mists, it was not the loveliness of these Spanish girls that set his pulses beating and sent the blood to his head. This was almost his first sight of gentlewomen since the memorable day in his native village, and the certainty that his opportunity had come at last filled him with both triumph and terror as he spurred down the slope, then paused and watched the cavalcade pick their way down through the golden grass and the thick green bush of the cañon. In a moment he recognised Don Enrique Ortega, who spoke to him pleasantly enough as he rode into the creek and dropped his bridle that his horse might drink. The two young men had met at the Mission, and although Enrique regarded the conquerors of his country as an inferior race, John was as good as any of them, and doubtless it was best to make no enemies. Moreover, his manners were very good.

'Ah, Don Juan,' he exclaimed, 'you have make the visit to Yerba Buena – San Francisco you call him now, no? I go this morning to meet my friends who make for the Rancho de los Olivos so great an honour. Si you permit me I introduce you, for you are the friend de my cousin, Padre Ortega.'

The company had scattered down the stream to refresh their horses, making a long banner of colour in the dark cañon. Don Enrique led John along the line, and presented him solemnly to each in turn. The caballeros protested eternal friendship with vehement insincerity, and the girls flashed their eyes and teeth at the blue-eyed young American without descending from their unconscious pride of sex and race. They had the best blood of Spain in them, and an American was an American, be he never so agreeable to contemplate.

The girls looked much alike in the rebosos which framed their faces so closely, and John promptly fell in love with all of them at once. Selection could take place later; he was too happy to think of anything so serious as immediate marriage. But one of them he determined to have.

He rode out of the cañon with them, and they were gracious, and chattered of the pleasures to come at the Rancho de los Olivos.

John noticed that Enrique kept persistently at the side of one maiden, and rode a little ahead with her. She was very tall and slim, and so graceful that she swayed almost to her horse's neck when branches drooped too low. John began to wish for a glimpse of her face.

'That is Delfina Carillo,' said the girl beside him, following his gaze. 'She go to marry with Enrique, I theenk. He is very devot, and I think she like him, but no will say.'

Perhaps it was merely the fact that this dainty flower hung a little higher than the others that caused John's thoughts to concentrate upon her, and roused his curiosity to such an extent that he drew his companion on to talk of the girl who was favoured by Enrique Ortega. He learned that she was the daughter of a great rancher near Santa Barbara, and was La Favorita of all the country round.

'She have the place that Chonita Iturbi y Moncada have before, and many caballeros want to marry with her, but she no pay much attention; only now I think like Enrique. Ay, he sing so beautiful, Señor, no wonder si she loving him. Serenade her every night, and she love the musica.'

'It certainly must be that,' thought John, 'for he hasn't an idea in his head.'

He did not see her until that night. The priest wore the brown robe of his order to the ball, and John his claw-hammer. They both looked out of place among those birds of brilliant plumage.

Doña Martina, large and coffee-coloured, with a mustache and many jewels, sat against the wall with other señoras of her kind. They wore heavy red and yellow satins, but the girls wore light silks that fluttered as they walked.

Doña Martina gave him a sleepy welcome, and he turned his attention to the dancing, in which he could take no part. He knew that his manners were good and his carriage easy, but the lighter graces had not come his way.

At the moment a girl was dancing alone in the middle of the *sala*, and John knew instinctively that she was Delfina Carillo. Like the other girls, she wore her hair high under a tall comb, but her gown was white and trimmed with the lace of Spain. Her feet, of course, were tiny, and showed plainly beneath her slightly lifted skirts; and she danced with no perceptible effort, rather as if swayed by a light wind, like the pendent moss in the woods. She had just begun to dance when John entered, and the company was standing against the wall in silence; but in a few moments the young men began to mutter, then to clap and stamp, then to shout, and finally they plunged their hands wildly into their pockets and flung gold and silver at her feet. But she took no notice beyond a flutter of nostril, and continued to dance like a thing of light and air.

Her beauty was very great. John, young as he was, knew that it was hardly likely he should ever see beauty in such perfection again. It was not an intellectual face, but it was faultless of line and

delicate of colouring. The eyes were not only very large and black,
but the lashes were so long and soft the wonder was they did not
tangle. Her skin was white, her cheeks and lips were pink, her
mouth was curved and flexible; and her figure, her arms and hands
and feet had the expression in their perfect lines that her face
lacked. John noticed that she had a short upper lip, a haughty
nostril, and a carriage that expressed pride both latent and active.
It was with an effort that she bent her head graciously as she
glided from the floor, taking no notice of the offerings that had
been flung at her feet.

And John loved her once and for all. She was the sublimation of
every dream that his romantic heart had conceived. He felt faint for a
moment at the difficulties which bristled between himself and this
superlative being, but he was a youthful conqueror, and life had been
very amiable to him. He shook courage into his spirit and asked to be
presented to her at once.

Her eyes swept his face indifferently, but something in his intense
regard compelled her attention, and although she appeared to scorn
conversation, she smiled once or twice; and when she smiled her face
was dazzling.

'That was very wonderful, that dance, señorita; but does it not
tire you?'

'No.'

'You are glad to give such great pleasure, I suppose?'

'Si – '

'You are so used to compliments – I know how the caballeros go
on – you won't mind my saying it was the most beautiful thing I ever
saw – and I have been about the world a bit.'

'Si?'

'I wish I could dance, if only to dance with you.'

'You no dance?' Her tone expressed polite scorn, although her
voice was scarcely audible.

'Would – would – you talk out a dance with me?'

'Oh no.' She looked as astonished as if John had asked her to shut
herself up alone in her room for the rest of the evening, and she
swayed her back slowly upon him and lifted her hand to the shoulder
of Enrique. In another moment she was gliding down the room in his
arm, and John noted that the colour in her cheek was deeper.

'It is impossible that she can care for that doll,' he thought;
'impossible.'

But in the days that followed he realised that the race was to be a hot one. He was included in all the festivities, and they went to *meriendas* among the cotton-woods by the river and in the hills, danced every night, were entertained by the priests at the Mission, and had bull-fights, horse-races, and many games of skill. Upon one occasion John was the happy host of a moonlight dance among his olive trees.

Enrique's attentions to his beautiful guest were persistent and unmistakable, and, moreover, he serenaded her nightly. John, riding about the ranch late, too restless to sleep, heard those dulcet tones raining compliments and vows upon Delfina's casement, and swore so furiously that he terrified the night birds.

But he, too, managed to keep close to Delfina, in spite of an occasional scowl from Enrique, who, however, held all Americans in too lofty a contempt to fear one. John had several little talks apart with her, and it was not long before he discovered that nature had done little for the interior of that beautiful shell. She had read nothing, and thought almost as little. What intelligence she had was occupied with her regalities, and although sweet in spite of her hauteur, and unselfish notwithstanding her good fortune, as a companion she would mean little to any man. John, however, was in the throes of his first passion, and his nature was ardent and thorough. Had she been a fool, simpering instead of dignified, he would not have cared. She was beautiful and magnetic, and she embodied an ideal. The ideal, however, or rather the ambition that was its other half, played no part in his mind as his love deepened. He wanted the woman, and had he suddenly discovered that she was a changeling born among the people, his love and his determination to marry her would have abated not a tittle.

His olive trees were neglected, and he spent the hours of their separations riding about the country with as little mercy on his horses as had he been a Californian born. Sometimes, touched by the youthful fervour in his eyes, Delfina would melt perceptibly and ask him a question or two about himself, a dazzling favour in one who held that words were made to rust. And once, when he lifted her off her horse under the heavy shadow of the trees, she gave him a glance which sent John far from her side, lest he make a fool of himself before the entire company. Meanwhile he was not unhappy, in spite of the wildness in his blood, for he found the tremors of love and hope and fear as sweet as they were extraordinary.

One evening the climax came.

Delfina expressed a wish to see the lake on the summit of the solitary peak. It had been discovered by the Indians, but was unknown to the luxurious Californians. The company was assembled on the long corridor traversing the front of the Casa Ortega when Delfina startled Enrique by a command to take them all to the summit that night.

'But, *señorita mia*,' exclaimed Enrique, turning pale at the thought of offending his goddess, 'there is no path. I do not know the way. And it is as steep as the tower of the Mission – '

John came forward. 'There is an Indian trail,' he said, 'and I have climbed it more than once. But it is very narrow – and steep, certainly.'

Delfina's eyes, which had flashed disdain upon Enrique, smiled upon John. 'We go with you,' she announced; 'tonight, for is moon. And I ride in front with you.'

On the whole, thought Talbot, glancing towards the great peak whose wilderness was still unrifled, that was the happiest night of his life. They outdistanced the others by a few yards, and they were obliged to ride so close that their shoulders touched. It was the full of the moon, but in the forest there was only an occasional splash of silver. They might have fancied themselves alone in primeval solitude had it not been for the gay voices behind them. And never had Delfina been so enchanting. She even talked a little, but her accomplished coquetry needed few words. She could express more by a bend of the head or an inflection of the voice than other women could accomplish with vocabularies and brains. John felt his head turning, but retained wisdom enough to wait for a moment when they should be quite alone.

The lake looked like a large reflection of the moon itself, for the black trees shadowed but the edge of the waters. So great was the beauty of the scene that for a few moments the company gazed at it silently, and the mountain-top remained as still as during its centuries of loneliness. But, finally, someone exclaimed, '*Ay, yi!*' and then rose a chorus, '*Dios de mi alma!*' '*Dios de mi vida!*' '*Ay*, California! California!' '*Ay, de mi, de mi, de mi!*'

Everybody, even Enrique, was occupied. John caught the bridle of Delfina's horse, and forced it back into the forest. And then his words tumbled one over the other.

'I must, I must!' he said wildly, keeping down his voice with difficulty. 'I've scarcely had a chance to make you love me, but I can't wait to tell you – I love you. I love you! I want to marry you! Oh –

I am choking!' He wrenched at his collar, and in truth he felt as if the very mountain were trembling.

Delfina had thrown back her head. 'Ay!' she remarked. Then she laughed.

She had no desire to be cruel, but her manifest amusement brought the blood down from John's head, and he shook from head to foot. His white face showed plainly in this fringe of the forest, and she ceased laughing and spoke kindly.

'Poor boy, I am sorry si I hurt you, but I no can marry you. Never I can love the Americano; no is like our men, so handsome, so graceful, so splendid. I like you, for are very nice boy, but I go to marry with Enrique. So no theenk more about it.' Then as he continued to stare, the youthful agony in his face touched her, and she leaned forward and said softly, 'Can kiss me once si you like. You are boy to me, no more, so I no mind.' And he kissed her with a violence of despair and passion which caused her maiden mind to wonder, and which she never experienced again.

He went no more to the Casa Ortega, and hid among his olive trees when the company clattered by the Mission. At the end of another week she returned to her home, and three months later she returned as the bride of Enrique Ortega.

Talbot smiled slightly as he recalled the sufferings of the boy long dead. There had been months when he had felt half-mad; then had succeeded several years of melancholy and a distaste for everything in life but work. He could not bring himself to sell the ranch and flee from the scene of his disappointment, for he was young enough to take a morbid pleasure in the very theatre of his failure.

He did not see Delfina again for three years. By that time she had three children and had begun to grow stout. But she was still very beautiful, and John kept out of her way for several years more.

But the years rolled round very swiftly. Doña Martina died. So did six of the ten children Delfina bore. Then Enrique died, leaving his diminished estates, his wife, and his four little girls to the care of John Talbot.

This was after fourteen years of matrimony and six years of intimacy between Talbot and the family of Los Olivos. One day Enrique, in desperation at the encroachments of certain squatters, had bethought himself of the American, now the most influential man in the county, and gone to him for advice. Talbot had found him a good lawyer, lent him the necessary money, and the squatters were dispossessed. Enrique's gratitude for Talbot knew no bounds;

he pressed the hospitality of Los Olivos upon him, and in time the two became fast friends.

Ortega and Delfina had jogged along very comfortably. She was an exemplary wife, a devoted mother, and as excellent a housekeeper as became her traditions. He made a kind and indulgent husband, and if neither found much to say to the other, their brief conversations were amiable. Enrique developed no wit with the years, but he was always a courteous host and played a good game of billiards, besides taking a mild interest in the affairs of the nation. John soon fell into the habit of spending two nights a week at the Rancho de los Olivos, and never failed to fill his pockets with sweets for the little girls, who preferred him to their father.

And his love! He used to fancy it was buried somewhere in the mausoleum of flesh which had built itself about Delfina Carillo. She weighed two hundred pounds, and her black hair and fine teeth were the only remnants of her splendid beauty. Her face was large and brown, and although she retained her dignity of carriage and moved with the old slow grace, she looked what she was, the Spanish mother of many children.

The change was gradual, and brought no pang with it. John's memory was a good one, and sometimes when it turned to his youth and the one passion of his life, he felt something like a sob in his soul, a momentary echo of the old agony. But it was only an echo; he had outgrown it all long since. He sometimes wondered that he loved no other woman, why his ambition to have an aristocratic wife had died with his first passion; and concluded that the intensity of his nature had worn itself out in that period of prolonged suffering, and that he was incapable of loving again. And the experience had satisfied him that marriage without love would be a poor affair. Once in a while, after leaving the plain coffee-coloured dame who filled the doorway as she waved him good-bye, he sighed as he recalled the exquisite creature of his youth. But these sighs grew less and less frequent, for not only was the grass high above that old grave in his heart and he a busy and practical man, but the Señora Ortega had become the most necessary of his friends. What she lacked in brain she made up in sympathy, and she had developed a certain amount of intelligence with the years. It became his habit to talk to her of all his ambitions and plans, particularly after the death of Enrique, when they had many uninterrupted hours together.

Upon Ortega's death Talbot took charge of the estate at once, and into the particulars of her handsome income it never occurred to the widow to enquire. One by one the girls married, and Talbot dowered them all. They were pretty creatures, and John loved them, for each had in her face a morsel of Delfina Carillo's lost beauty; and if they recalled the pain of his youth they recalled its sweetness too. The Señora recalled neither.

For the last year she had been quite alone. Two of her daughters lived in the city of Mexico. One had married a Spanish Consul and returned with him to Spain. The other lived in San Francisco, and as soon as domestic affairs would permit intended to visit her sisters. Talbot, when at home, called on the Señora once a week and always carried a novel or an illustrated paper in his saddle-bag.

'Is the tragedy at this end or the other?' thought Talbot, as he walked up and down the Mission corridor on his fortieth birthday – 'that I could not have her when I was mad about her, or that I can have her now and don't want her?'

He knew that the Señora was lonesome in her big house and would have welcomed a companion, but he knew also that the desire moved sluggishly in the depths of her lazy mind. If he were willing, well and good. If otherwise, it mattered not much.

His Indian servant cantered up with his horse, he gave a last regretful glance at the cool corridor of the Mission, and then went out into the hot sun.

He was only a stone heavier than in the old days, but he rode more slowly, for this his favourite mare was no longer young. His day for breaking in bucking mustangs was over, and he liked an animal that would behave itself as became the four-footed companion of his years.

The road through the pale green cotton-woods and willows that wooded the banks of the river – as dry as the heavens – was almost cold, and refreshingly dim; but when the bed and its fringe turned abruptly to the south his way led for five sweltering miles through sun-burned fields and over hills as yellow as polished gold. The sky looked like dark-blue metal in which a hole had been cut for a lake of fire. The heat it emptied quivered visibly in the parched fields, and the mountains swam in a purple haze. Talbot had a grape-leaf in his hat, and the suns of California had baked his complexion long since, but he wished that his birthday occurred in winter, as he had wished many a time before.

It was an hour and a half before he rode into the grounds surrounding Casa Ortega. Then he spurred his horse, for here were many old oak trees and the atmosphere was twenty degrees cooler. A Mexican servant met him, and he dismounted and walked the few remaining yards to the house. He sighed as he remembered that Herminia, the last of the girls to marry, had been there to kiss him on his last birthday. He would gladly have had all four back again, and now they had passed out of his life forever.

The Casa Ortega was a very long adobe house one storey in height and one room deep, except in an ell where a number of rooms were bunched together. The Señora had it whitewashed every year, and the red tiles on the roof renewed when necessary; therefore it had none of the pathetic look of old age peculiar to the adobe mansions of the dead grandees.

A long veranda traversed the front, supported by pillars and furnished with gaily painted chairs; but it was empty, and Talbot entered the *sala* at once. It was a long room, severely furnished in the old style, and facing the door was a painting of Delfina Carillo. Talbot rarely allowed his eyes to wander to this portrait. Had he dared he would have asked for its removal. The grass was long above the grave, but there were such things as ghosts.

The Señora was sitting in a corner of the dim cool room, and rose at once to greet him. She came forward with a grace and dignity of carriage that still had the power to prick his admiration. But she was very dark, and the old enchanting smile had lost its way long since in the large cheeks and heavy chin. Even her eyes no longer looked big, and the famous lashes had been worn down by many tears; for there were six little graves in the Ortega corner of the Mission churchyard, and she had loved her children devotedly. She carried her two hundred pounds as unconsciously as she had once carried her willowy inches, and she wore soft black cashmere in winter and lawn in summer, fastened at the throat with a miniature of the husband of her youth. She was only thirty-nine, but there was not a vestige of youth about her anywhere, and her whole being expressed a life lived, and a sleepy contentment with the fact. Talbot often wondered if she had no hours of insupportable loneliness; but she gave no sign, and he concluded that novels and religion sufficed.

'So hot it is, no?' she said in her soft hardly audible tones, that, like her carriage and manner, were unchanged. 'You have the face very red, but feel better in a little while. Very cool here, no?'

'I feel ten years younger than I did a quarter of an hour ago. There was a time – alas! – when I could stand the suns of California for six hours at a stretch, but – '

'Ay, yes, we grow more old every year. Is twenty now since we *merienda* all day and dance all night – when I am a visitor here, no more; and you are the thin boy with the long arms, and legs, and try to grow the mustache.'

It was the first time she had ever referred to their youth, and he stared at her. But her face was as placid as if she had been helping him to chicken with chilli-sauce, and he wondered if it could change. Involuntarily he glanced at the portrait. It seemed alive with expression, and – the room was almost dark – he fancied the eyes were tragic.

'How can she stand it?' he thought. 'How *can* she?'

'You are improve,' she continued politely. 'The American mens no grow old like the Spanish – or like the women that have ten children and get so stout and have the troubles – '

'You have retained much, Señora,' exclaimed Talbot, blundering over the first compliment he had paid her in twenty years.

She smiled placidly and moved her head gently; the word 'shake' could never apply to any of her movements. 'I have the mirror – and the picture. And I no mind, Don Juan. When the woman bury the six children, no care si she grow old. The more soon grow old the more soon die and see the little ones – am always very fond of Enrique also,' she added, 'but when am young love more. He is very good man always, but he grow old like myself and very fat. Only you are improve, my friend. That one reason why always I am so glad to see you. Remind me of that time when all are young and happy.'

Old Marcia announced dinner, and Talbot sprang to his feet with a sensation of relief and offered the Señora his arm. She made no further references to their youth during the excellent and highly seasoned repast, but discussed the possibilities of the crops and listened with deep attention to the political forecast. She knew that politics were becoming the absorbing interest in the life of her friend, and although she also knew that they would one day put a continent between herself and him, she had long since ceased to live for self, and never failed to encourage him.

When the last *dulce* had been eaten they went out upon the veranda and talked drowsily of minor matters until both nodded in their comfortable chairs, and finally fell asleep.

For a time the heavy dinner locked Talbot's brain, but finally he began to dream of his youth, and the scenes of which Delfina Carillo had been the heroine were flung from their rusty frames into the hot light of his memory, until he lived again the ecstasy and the anguish of that time. The morning's reminiscences had moved coldly in his mind, but so intense was his vision of the woman he had worshipped that she seemed bathed in light.

He awoke suddenly. The Señora still slept, and her face was as placid as in consciousness. It was slightly relaxed, but the time had not yet come for the pathetic loss of muscular control. Still, she looked so large and brown and stout that Talbot rose abruptly with an echo of the agony that had returned in sleep, and entered the *sala* and stood deliberately before the portrait. It had been painted by an artist of much ability. There was atmosphere behind it, which in the dim room detached it from the canvas; and the curved red mouth smiled, the eyes flashed with the triumph of youth and much conquest, the skin was as white as the moon-flowers in the fields at night.

Talbot recalled the night he had taken this woman in his arms – not the woman on the veranda – and involuntarily he raised them to the picture. 'And I thought it was over,' he muttered, with a terrified gasp. 'But I believe I would give my immortal soul and everything I've accomplished in life if she would come out of the frame and the past for an hour and love me.'

'Whatte you say?' drawled a gentle voice. 'I fall asleep, no? Si you ring that little bell Marcia bring the chocolate. You find it too hot out here?'

'Oh, no; I prefer it out of doors. It is cooler now, and I like all the air I can get.'

He longed to get away, but he sipped his chocolate and listened to the domestic details of his four vicarious daughters. The Señora was immensely proud of her five grandchildren. Their photographs were all over the house.

At six o'clock he shook hands with her and sprang on his horse. Half-way down the avenue he turned his head, as usual. She stood on the veranda still, and smiled pleasantly to him, moving one of her large brown hands a little. He never saw the Señora again.

2

Talbot was obliged to go to San Francisco a day or two later, and when he returned the Señora was in bed with a severe cold. He sent her a box of books and papers, and another of chocolates, and then forgot her in the excitement of the elections. It was the autumn of the year 1868, and he was an enthusiastic admirer of Grant. He

stumped the State for that admirable warrior and indifferent states-
man, with the result that his own following increased; and his interest
in politics waxed with each of several notable successes in behalf of
the candidate. He finally announced decisively that he should run
for Congress at the next elections, and a member of the House
of Representatives from his district dying two days later, he was
appointed at once to fill the vacant chair.

The Señora was still in bed with a persistent cold and cough when
he left for Washington late in November, but he rode over to leave a
goodbye with old Marcia, and ordered a bookseller in San Francisco
to send her all the illustrated papers and magazines.

She entered his mind but seldom during those interesting months
in Washington. Talbot became sure of his particular talent at
last, and determined to remain in politics for the rest of his life.
Moreover, the excitement until the 4th of March was intense, for
Southern blood was still hot and bitter, and there were rumours in the
air that Grant would be assassinated on the day of his inauguration.
He was not, however, and Talbot was glad to be in Washington on
that memorable day. He wrote the Señora an account both of the
military appearance of the city and of the brilliant scene in the Senate
Chamber, but she had ceased, for the time, to be a weekly necessity
in his life.

And being a bachelor, wealthy, handsome, and properly launched,
he was soon skimming that social sea of many crafts. For the first
time since his abrupt severance from the Los Olivos festivities he
enjoyed society. San Francisco's had seemed a poor imitation of what
novels described, but Washington was full of brilliant interest. And
he met more than one woman who recalled his boyish ideals, women
who were far more like the vision in the English churchyard than
Delfina Carillo; who, indeed, had not resembled the English girl in
anything but manifest of race, and had been an ideal apart, never to
be encountered again in this world.

It was a long and exciting session, and he gave all the energies of
his mind to the great question of reconstruction, but more than once
he asked himself if the time had not come to marry, if it were not a
duty to his old self to gratify the ambition to which he owed the
foundations of his success with life. A beautiful and high-bred wife
would still afford him profound satisfaction, no doubt of that. He
could in the last ten or twelve years have married more than one
charming San Francisco girl, but that interval of passionate love
between his youthful ambition and his many opportunities had given

him a distaste for a lukewarm marriage. Here in Washington, however, California seemed a long way off, and he was only forty, in the
very perfection of mental and physical vigour. Could he not love
again? Surely a man in the long allotted span must begin life more
than once. He found himself, after an hour, in some beautiful
woman's boudoir, or with a charming girl in the pale illumination of
a conservatory, longing for the old tremors of hope and despair,
and he determined to let himself go at the first symptom. But he
continued to be merely charmed and interested. If the turbulent
waters were in him still, they had fallen far below their banks and
would not rise at his bidding.

It was not to be expected that the Señora would write; she hated
the sight of a pen, and only wrote once a month – with sighs of
protest that were almost energetic – to her daughters. Padre Ortega
was too old for correspondence; consequently Talbot heard no news
of Santa Ursula except from his major-domo, who wrote a monthly
report of the progress of the olive trees and the hotel. This person
was not given to gossip, and Talbot was in ignorance of the health of
his old friend, in spite of one or two letters of enquiry, until almost
the end of the session. Then the major-domo was moved to write the
following postscript to one of his dry reports:

> The Señora is dying, I guess – consumption, the galloping kind.
> You may see her again, and you mayn't. We're all sorry here, for
> she's always bin square and kind.

There still remained three weeks of the session, but Talbot's
committee had finished its work, and he was practically free. He
paired with a friendly Democrat, and started for California the
day he received the letter. The impulse to go to the bedside of his
old friend had been immediate and peremptory. He forgot the
pleasant women in Washington, his new-formed plans. The train
seemed to walk.

They were not sentimental memories that moved so persistently in
his mind during that long hot journey overland. Had they risen they
would have been rebuked, as having no place in the sad reality of
today. An old friend was dying, the most necessary and sympathetic
he had known. He realised that she had become a habit, and that
when she left the world he would be very much alone. His mind
dwelt constantly on that large brown kindly presence, and he winked
away more than one tear as he reflected that he should go to her no
more for sympathy, do nothing further to alleviate the loneliness of

her life. In consequence he was in no way prepared for what awaited him at Los Olivos.

He arrived at night. Padre Ortega was away, so he could get no news of the Señora except that she was still alive. He sent her a note at once, telling her to expect him at eleven the next morning.

Again he took a long hot ride over sun-burned hills and fields, for it wanted but a few weeks of his birthday. As he cantered through the oaks near the house he saw that a hammock was swung across the veranda, and that someone lay in it – a woman, for a heavy braid of black hair hung over the side and trailed on the floor.

'Surely,' he thought, 'surely – it cannot be the Señora – in a hammock!' And then he suddenly realised that the disease must have taken her flesh.

His hands trembled as he dismounted and tied his horse to a tree, and he lingered as long as he could, for he felt that his face was white. But he was a man long used to self-control, and in a moment he walked steadily forward and ascended the steps to the veranda. And then as he stood looking down upon the hammock he needed all the control he possessed.

For the Señora had gone and Delfina Carillo lay there. Not the magnificent pulsing creature of old, for her face was pinched and little blue veins showed everywhere; but the ugly browns had gone with her flesh, her skin was white, and her cheeks flamed with colour. Her eyes looked enormous, and her mouth had regained its curves and mobility, although it drooped. She wore a soft white wrapper with much lace about the throat; and she looked twenty-six, and beautiful, wreck as she was.

'Delfina!' he articulated. 'Delfina!' And then he sat down, for his knees were shaking. The blood seemed rushing through his brain, and after that first terrible but ecstatic moment of recognition, he was conscious of a poignant regret for the loss of his brown old friend. He glanced about, involuntarily. Where had she gone – that other personality? For even the first soul of the woman looked from the great eyes in the hammock.

Delfina stared at him for some moments, without speaking. Then she said, with a sigh, 'Ay – it is Juan.'

She sat up abruptly. 'Listen,' she said, speaking rapidly. 'At first I no know you, for the mind wander much; and then Marcia tell me I think always I am the girl again. Sometimes, even when I have the sense, I theenk so too, for am alone, have nothing to remind, and I like theenk that way. When I am seeck first Herminia coming to see me, but I write her, after, am well again, for I know she and the husband want to go to Mexico. Then, after I get worse, I am very glad she going, that all my girls are away; for the dreams I have when the mind is no right give me pleasure and bring back the days when am young and so happy. I feel glad I go to die that way and not like the old peoples. So happy I am sometimes, Juan, you cannot theenk! Was here, you remember, for two months before I marry, and often I see you and Enrique and all my friends, and myself so gay and beautiful, and all the caballeros so crazy for me, and all the splendid costumes and horses. Ay California! Her youth, too, is gone, Juan! Never she is Arcadia again.' She paused, but did not lie down, and in a few moments went on: 'And often I theenk of you – often. So strange, for love Enrique then; but – I no know – missing you terreeblay when you go to Washington, and read all they say about you in the papers. So long now since Enrique going, and the love go long before – the love that make me marry him, I mean, for always love the husband; that was my duty. So, when my youth come back, though I think some by Enrique, suppose you are more in the mind, which, after all, is old, though much fall away. And I want, want to see you, but no like to ask you to come, for you are so busy and so ambeetious, and I know I live till you come again si is a year, and that make me feel happy. No cry, my friend. I no cry, for is sweet to be young again. Often I no can understand why not loving you then; you are so fine man now – but was boy then, and I admeer so much the caballeros, so splendid, and talk so graceful; no was use then to the other kind. But, although I no theenk much before – have so many babies and so much trouble, and, after, nothing no matter – always I feel deep down I have miss something in life; often I sigh, but no know why. But theenk much when go to die, and now I know that si I am really young again, and well, I marry you and am happy in so many ways with you, and have the intelligence. Never I really have been alive. I know that now.'

She fell back, panting a little, and her voice, always very low, had become almost inaudible. She motioned to a bottle of angelica on the table beside her, and John took her in his arms and put the glass to her lips. It brought the colour back to her face, and she lifted her arms and crossed them behind his neck.

'Juan,' she whispered coaxingly, 'you have love me once – I know, and sometimes have cried, because theenk how I have made you suffer. Make the believe I am really the young girl again, and love me like then. Going very soon now – and will make me very happy.'

'It is easy enough to imagine,' he said; 'easy enough! It will be a ghastly travesty, God knows, but could I have foreseen today during that terrible time, I would have welcomed it as better than nothing.'